A holiday gift for readers of
Harlequin American Romance

Novellas from three of your favorite authors

Four Texas Babies

Tina Leonard

A Texan Under the Mistletoe

Leah Vale

Merry Texmas

Linda Warren

CHRISTMAS, Texas Style

Tina Leonard

Leah Vale

Linda Warren

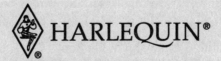

HARLEQUIN®

TORONTO • NEW YORK • LONDON
AMSTERDAM • PARIS • SYDNEY • HAMBURG
STOCKHOLM • ATHENS • TOKYO • MILAN • MADRID
PRAGUE • WARSAW • BUDAPEST • AUCKLAND

ISBN 0-373-75093-5

CHRISTMAS, TEXAS STYLE

Copyright © 2005 by Harlequin Books S.A.

The publisher acknowledges the copyright holders of the individual works as follows:

FOUR TEXAS BABIES
Copyright © 2005 by Tina Leonard.

A TEXAN UNDER THE MISTLETOE
Copyright © 2005 by Leah Vroman.

MERRY TEXMAS
Copyright © 2005 by Linda Warren.

www.eHarlequin.com

Printed in U.S.A.

CONTENTS

FOUR TEXAS BABIES
Tina Leonard

Dear Reader,

Christmas is such a wonderful, family time of year. In our home we practically have the Christmas tree up and the menorah on the mantel when the Halloween trick-or-treaters hit the doorstep. This year the tree went up November first, because I couldn't wait to start the holiday season!

The holidays get their big kickoff for us at Thanksgiving, when I have as much family over as possible. It's the one time of year the china comes out of storage to be placed on the table!

Then the serious business of holiday decorating begins. In organized years I've done my shopping before November; most years we're "finishing up" a week into December.

My favorite part of the holidays, though, is when my children are finished school for the semester. That's when Christmas *really* begins for me. And I stretch the season until New Year's, when I have tons of friends over to visit all day with us, in an effort to stave off the fact that my children must return to school, and a new session must begin.

I love the holiday season, and I hope that you and yours have a wonderfully blessed and joyous time with *your* families and friends.

Love,

Tina Leonard

Many thanks to Paula Eykelhof for allowing me to do this anthology, and to Stacy Boyd and Kathleen Scheibling for being such supportive editors.

Nothing in my life is possible without my friends— you know who you are. I hope this holiday season brings you, and all my wonderful readers, great joy and peace.

Lisa and Dean, I love you.
This year we bake cookies for Christmas.

Chapter One

July 1

Dear Sam,
The Bartholomews have made us an offer we cannot refuse, although we never imagined we might one day sell to folks we don't particularly like. That being said, we have to play the hand we are dealt. You don't seem to want to settle, and Phin doesn't want to work the ranch. We have agreed to sell to the Bartholomews by Christmas of this year—if it appears neither of you intends to take over the reins. Hopefully, the closing date we have managed to negotiate will give you time to discover what is really in your heart. Love, Mom and Dad

P.S. Even though you're thirty-three, it's not too late to settle down, marry a good girl like Mary Phillips who understands ranch life, and start a family.

Sam Johnston drove into Union Junction, Texas, on a day black and windy enough to match the sadness in his heart. The last thing he wanted to do was return to Montana, but his brother Phin had made sure their parents' letter had reached him. Sam had been riding in a rodeo, and though his wrist ached from a twist he'd taken on a bounty bull that had meant business, his pride and his heart hurt more right now.

It bothered him that his parents felt their golden years depended upon his return to Falling Hills Ranch. He would have liked a little more time to figure out what was best for himself and for his family.

His younger brother, of course, was playing devil's speed bump, trying to keep his parents from sticking him with the responsibilities. At twenty-nine, Phin wasn't about to wear the family saddle of responsibility.

Phin was the point on the triangle between his parents and Sam. Phin liked living in Montana, he liked the ranch and he could easily take it over. But his brother wanted Sam to handle the business matters so that Phin could chase his dream of starting a ski resort or a golf course.

Would Phin take charge if Sam stayed on the road? Sam doubted it. Phin mainly took care of Phin.

Sam sighed, parking his truck and drumming his fingers on the steering wheel as he looked at the Union Junction Hair Salon. He needed time to think, and this stop between nowhere and Montana was good enough. A haircut, some lunch and maybe a beer with the locals might take the burn out of his mood.

He really enjoyed traveling the country, soaking up every town's characteristics. He wasn't ready to be tied to one place, one way of life, or even one woman.

In Montana, if a man was going to survive, it was best to have a woman if for no other reason than to cook food and share some body heat.

He frowned. Even if settling down *wasn't* such a bad thing, Mary Phillips would not be his choice, despite his parents' broad hint about his high school sweetheart. It was true Mary understood ranch life, but how could a gentle soul like Mary understand him?

The wily ace in the hole of his parents' letter was the offer from the Bartholomews. Could his folks possibly be serious about selling out to such scurvy, no-good, dime-store cowboys?

If two families despised each other more than the Hatfields and McCoys, it was the Johnstons and the Bartholomews. The Bartholomews would keep the best part of the huge Falling Hills Ranch for themselves, then carve the rest up into profitable condo and retail sites. They weren't above cutting deals with the state for use of their land—in return for power and position. In short, they were belly-crawlers who hid under a ranching family's hat for the sake of money and tax breaks.

"Hey, cowboy," a voice called, interrupting his thoughts.

He glanced up at the tiny blonde staring at him from the porch of the salon. Getting out of the truck, he shut the door and tipped his hat to her. "Ma'am."

"It's miss," she said. "Come on in and have a glass of tea, traveler. We don't bite in here."

"Nobody said you did," he said mildly. "I'm just trying to decide if I want a trim or not."

She shrugged. "You can get one of those in Montana. Or here. Suit yourself."

His family was well known in ranching towns, even as far south as Texas. And he was often recognized from his rodeo career. His truck door was emblazoned with the family business name and logo, so she was paying attention. But she was just a bit too spunky for him. "Do you work or just run your mouth?"

She sized him up as he stepped onto the porch. "Hello, Sam Johnston," she said. "My name's Lily. And I multitask, as most hairdressers do."

"More cut and less lip, that's all I'm looking for," he said crossly.

"Fine." She pointed the way inside, looking mighty fine, he noticed, in worn blue jeans and a white blouse. "I've never had an unhappy customer."

That might change right now, Sam thought. His mood stunk. He hadn't fully digested the contents of his parents' letter, and even if he had, he'd still be in a grumpy mood. Sitting in the chair she indicated, Sam winced when she picked up scissors.

It was the gleam in her eye that made him cautious. "I'm not certain you're trustworthy."

Her smile was nothing short of Mona Lisa's as she put the scissors on the table again.

"What are you doing?" he demanded.

"Waiting for you to take off your hat. As good a stylist as I am, I can't cut hair around your Stetson."

He grunted, removing his hat. "Did I tell you I just wanted a *little* taken off?"

His gaze met hers in the mirror. Lily ran her hand through his hair. Her touch felt wonderful, he was annoyed to discover, and he liked her confident demeanor.

In fact, an irritating bulge was growing under the zipper of his jeans, and he wasn't happy about it. "I knew of a Lily once, a long time ago."

She looked at him. "Did you?"

"It's not a very common name."

"Hmm. How do you expect me to cut your hair if you keep talking?" she asked.

"I thought you multitask." He shifted, placing his hat in his lap, glad for the cover.

She touched the uneven strands of his hair. "I presume you did the work yourself?"

He nodded. "Maybe I shouldn't quit my regular job."

"Not if you're better at it."

"I'm not sure if I am or not." He sighed, the prospect of losing his regular rodeo work for the ranching life weighing heavy on his mind. "So I guess you hear a lot from your clients."

"A lot I'll never tell, cowboy." She gave him a curious look in the mirror. "Hairdresser-client privilege."

He had to tell somebody. His mind was on fire and his heart was torn. She was as safe as anyone. Heck, Lily probably wasn't even her real name. This woman could not possibly be the girl he'd heard of when he was younger. She'd been the daughter of his family's arch enemies—or rivals, if one wanted to be gentle about it. Lily was reputed to be spoiled. She'd grown up with all the luxuries her family, the Bartholomews, could give her. From what he'd heard, they'd also taught her the same belly-crawler-hiding-under-a-ranching-hat tricks they thrived on.

But this hairdresser seemed professional and responsible, though a bit too sassy for his tastes. His gaze met hers just as a much bigger chunk of hair than he was comfortable losing hit the floor.

"Sorry," she said, "you really butchered it. I'm trying to be conservative, but it's very uneven."

Well, she was forthright. "Hey, would you charge me extra for an opinion?"

She shook her head. "Hairdressers listen. They don't give more opinion than a 'Mmm, you don't say. Did she really do that, hon? How do you survive?' kind of thing. At least that's my schtick."

He really wanted one person's opinion, just one person who lived outside his family. And though he'd known her only for a few minutes, there was just something about her. He felt as if he could trust Lily. "My folks want me married."

She nodded. "Most parents want to see their children happy."

"I'm not so sure marriage would make me happy." He frowned. "Especially not to Mary Phillips."

The scissors, which were poised to cut, stayed still.

"What's wrong?" he asked.

"Nothing." She returned to scrutinizing his hair. "There, all finished."

He stared at her. "You just started!"

"You said you wanted a trim. That's what you got." She put her scissors away.

Feeling his hair, he had to admit that the back was smoother. And it was still long, the way he liked it. But he wasn't through talking to her! "How much do I owe you? Can I talk you into dinner?"

She shook her head as he rose. "No, but thank you, anyway. And the cut is twenty-five. I'm giving you a discount since you're passing through town."

"Thanks." He dug out his wallet and gave her fifty bucks. Then he quickly spat out his dilemma, just to see if she could help. "If I don't settle down very quickly, my folks are going to sell our family ranch to some low-down, scurvy, good-for-nothing people."

"Really?" Lily put the money in her pocket and looked at him. "Who?"

"The Bartholomews," Sam said.

LILY BARTHOLOMEW HAD known who the darkly handsome cowboy was the moment he'd parked his truck with the Johnston ranch logo on the door in front of the salon. She'd seen him ride in rodeos, and knew she wasn't the first woman to think he was hotter than a Texas sunrise.

What she hadn't known was just how much he despised her family. It was clear by the look in his dark eyes that he was down and needed a listening ear—yet it couldn't be hers. "Are they as bad as you think they are?"

"Yeah. But nothing I can't handle, if I was interested in taking over the family ranch. I just don't think I am."

This was getting far too personal. In other circumstances, she might not mind, but if he discovered that she was a Bartholomew, he'd feel tricked. "Cowboy, I have another appointment."

"I apologize." Glancing around, he said, "Now?"

"In a few moments." She looked up at him defiantly. "I do appreciate the tip, however. You didn't have to be quite so generous. Your hair wasn't in that bad a shape."

He grinned at her. "Have dinner with me. I can show you the real meaning of generous."

Her eyes widened. If he was any other man, she might be tempted to say yes. He was packing an awful lot of temptation into that smile. She shivered. "You make it hard to say no, but I'm afraid I must."

"Your six o'clock just canceled, Lily," someone called from another room. "You're done for the night."

"Here we go," Sam said, taking her by the arm and escorting her from the room. "Dinner with a stranger."

"No," she said, laughing in spite of herself. "Sam, it's a really bad idea."

"Because you never cross that hairdresser-client line?"

He was smiling down at her, his grin a lazy, crooked crescent, and Lily's heart jumped in spite of herself. "I never have, that's true."

"Good. I've never dated a woman who cut my hair, either. Then again, you are the sexiest stylist to tame it."

She stared up at him, wanting to accept his offer, and maybe make a few of her own. Should she tell him who her family was? Clear it up right now, and see if he still offered dinner? "Sam—"

"I'm in the mood to drive," he said.

"Drive? You just got into town."

"I know. But I heard there's a barbecue tonight at a ranch called Malfunction Junction—"

"No," Lily said. She didn't want her friends, the Jefferson brothers, to spill the beans about who she was. At least not until she was ready to tell. "How about we take a picnic out into the country?"

He smiled, and she thought she saw the hint of a wolf light his face. "Sounds good to me."

"Great. This will please all of us. Follow me."

"All of us?" He did as she asked, following her into the upstairs of the salon.

She opened her bedroom door, and a giant golden retriever bounded off her bed to greet her and inspect him. "Meet Samson. Our latest rescued pet. The stylists here run an animal-rescue business on the side."

He grimaced as Samson put hairy paws on his chest, looking up at Sam. "Down, young lad."

She laughed. Dragging him off of Sam, she showed the delighted dog to her bed. "We just got him last week, and I'm not sure I'm going to be able to let him go. He seems to have adopted me."

"Very comfortable," Sam observed. "If that was my bed, I'd probably stay, too."

Lily felt herself blush. "Well, Samson will come along on our picnic. You'd be surprised what a good listener he is. You can tell him anything."

Not to mention that Samson would provide a chaperone of sorts. She put a leash on the dog and handed him to Sam. "If you don't mind doing the honors, I'll pack the picnic."

"If you rescued him, where's his family?"

"We're not sure. He might have run away or he might have been dumped. He's very friendly and still a junior dog, so he could have gotten nosy and kept on going, not realizing he was getting lost. But it doesn't matter. He has a home with me for as long as he needs."

"You are one lucky pup," Sam told the dog.

He might not think that if she told him it was her parents his ranch might be sold to. But she'd decided not to think about that, at least not until she'd spent a little more time with this too-tempting man. "Water, fruit, some crackers, and even a candy bar," she said, packing the food into a picnic basket. "That's just about perfect."

"Yes, it is," Sam said. "When I stopped here tonight, I didn't imagine I'd be having this much fun."

She turned, looking into those dark brown eyes of his. "That's an awfully nice thing to say."

"I'm not being polite, Lily of Union Junction," he said. "I really do feel like luck will be my lady tonight."

Chapter Two

To Sam's surprise, he never once felt another need to talk about his parents' startling news, and Lily never asked. They played Frisbee with Samson, and ate the picnic she'd prepared. Lily was surprisingly open with him. He was, after all, a stranger. Except for his rodeo expertise, she knew nothing about him.

"I'm sorry I'm only going to be here tonight," he said as they lay on the picnic blanket, staring up at the stars with a fully worn-out Samson beside them. "This is the most fun I've had in a long time."

"More fun than rodeo?" Lily asked.

"Absolutely." He rolled on his side to look at her. "I like to travel. I think I like avoiding being tied down to the ranch."

"I can understand that," Lily said. "I left home a long time ago."

"Marriage?" He hoped she didn't have a sad story to tell. She seemed like such a sweet lady. Had she known a lot of happiness in her life?

"No," Lily said softly. "Just had to make my own way."

"Got folks somewhere?" He wasn't sure why he asked. It was none of his business. Something about her made him want to get to know her better—a lot better.

Until his parents had reminded him of Mary Phillips, he

hadn't realized how very few females he'd interacted with. Or how he hadn't had a long-term relationship with a woman— or anyone except his family.

"I have folks," she said, "but we're not all that close."

He watched a star that seemed to burn brighter for an instant. "Hey, if you had a ranch, and you needed to get married to make your folks happy so they wouldn't sell it, would you do it?"

She laid a soft hand on his arm. "Hairdressers listen," she said. "It's my policy not to give many opinions. Particularly to strangers. Too many wrong answers could cost me clientele."

He laughed. "You and Samson seem to be doing fine."

"For a couple of strays, we're doing all right."

There was tension in her tone. Sam laid his hand over the one she'd placed on his arm, surprised when she didn't draw away. "Being a stray has served me well most of my life. Now I've got to find myself a home, I suppose."

"Well, I only take in animals, or I'd offer," Lily said with a smile.

"Too bad. I did like the look of your bed. Of course, Samson has already staked it out as his."

"Yes." She removed her hand, and he immediately missed her warmth. "I should be getting back."

Like the star, he'd felt himself burn brighter at her touch. If they left now, left this magical place that seemed to be just for the two of them, he knew he would never touch her again. "What do you want most in life?"

"I can't say, Sam. Stylists don't waste their clients' time talking about themselves. Well, the good ones don't."

"You sure do have a lot of rules."

She smiled at him. "Just keeping my distance."

"And very well at that." He raised a brow at her. "But this is cowboy/new-friend privilege. And I'd never tell a secret you shared with me."

"All right," she said, her tone reluctant but hopeful, almost as if she wanted to tell him something. "I'd like real independence."

"Isn't all independence real?"

Her hazel eyes lit on him, and he found himself wanting to run his fingers through her long, honey-blond hair.

"My folks always made me feel as if I hadn't measured up to their idea of success because I didn't settle...close to them," she said. "If I'd been a proper daughter, I would have made a good match and settled down. Not left for Texas and become a hairdresser."

Sam straightened. "That's almost word for word what I'm up against."

"The problem is," Lily said, "I don't agree with my folks on much of anything. We're too different. And I think I went my own way just so I wouldn't give in. It looked like a long, lonely road of nothing if I did things their way." She sighed. "Not every girl's idea of happiness is to marry the man their folks pick out for them."

"You could marry me," Sam said. "Then we'd both be out of the ditch."

Lily laughed. "You have no idea how impossible that is."

"Why?" Sam scooted next to her, taking her hand in his. "You don't know me, I don't know you. It would be one of those arranged-marriage things. We could even do up a contract. If I get married," he said, "my parents won't sell the ranch to the Bartholomews."

"Really?"

"Yes. I believe in my heart they'd rather live out their days on the ranch. They probably have twenty more years of happiness in front of them. No place says home to them more than Falling Hills. But I'll admit it's too much responsibility for them now. They're just hedging their bets with this ultimatum." He took a deep breath. "I don't blame them for think-

ing they might as well get out from underneath something neither Phin nor I have wanted much to do with."

"Don't you, though? It sounds like a wonderful place."

He smiled. "It is wonderful. I'm only being stubborn, I suppose, because like you, it looked long and lonely committing
to the lifetime of hard ranching my father knew. I wanted my
years of roaming."

"And now they want grandchildren."

He looked at her, his heart suddenly beating hard. Taking
the letter from his pocket, he read over it again, his feelings
of panic the same as when he'd read it the first time. "You're
right. It's the final thing they mention. Maybe that's what they
need to make them happy, to keep them on the ranch a little
longer, until I figure out what I really want to do." He looked
at the letter again. "Yes, it's in there. Start a family. See?"

"No, thank you," Lily said, drawing back so he couldn't
hand her the letter. "Hairdressers never read personal corre-
spondence addressed to other people."

Grinning, he said, "Do they get married on a whim?"

"About fifty percent do, I'm sure," Lily said, "though there
are no real statistics on it."

"Lily," he said, leaning gently against her so that she rolled
onto her back, "do you kiss a man you've only just met?"

"I might," she said, "if the man is you."

"Good." He kissed her so long and deep he knew beyond
a shadow of a doubt that she was just as attracted to him as
he was to her. "Wow," he said, after he'd pulled away, "cutting hair isn't the only thing you're good at."

"Come here, cowboy," she said, pulling him close to her
again, "use those lips for something besides talking."

SAM WAS THE SEXIEST MAN she'd come across in a long time.
In fact, he was the sexiest man she'd ever met.

She discounted the notion of forbidden fruit. Sure, her parents would be angry if they knew she was in any way Sam's girl, but she wasn't doing this to have a laugh on her parents.

His kisses simply were too hot, and the feelings racing around inside her right now had nothing to do with her parents' feud. He made her feel things she'd never felt before. He made her think even her wildest dreams might really be possible.

Tonight, it would be just her and Sam. Nothing in the past mattered. Until they left this spot, that's the way she was going to think of it.

"Don't stop kissing me," she murmured, when he looked down at her.

"You are a crazy little thing," he said.

"Just because this is too good."

He chuckled. "Almost like we've known each other forever."

They had, sort of, but he didn't need to know that. "Why didn't I meet you before?" she asked.

"Before what?"

She blinked. "Before I became the black sheep of the family."

He laughed, stroking her hair away from her face as she looked up at him. "Lily, even your name is pure and clean. I doubt very seriously that anything about you is dark and sinister." Tugging at her bottom lip with his, he slid his tongue inside her mouth, sweeping her with a hot kiss that expertly drew a moan from her. Her fingers tightened on his arms, and suddenly she knew that all her life she had allowed her parents to rule her, even from afar.

But this man she could have for herself. It didn't matter who he was, not with what he was offering. It didn't matter that she was the black sheep, because he didn't know who she was.

And it wouldn't hurt him if he didn't know, because what he wanted was oh, so simple. When he caressed along her arms and her breasts, she took a deep breath and jumped for the abyss. "Why would a girl want an arranged marriage with you?"

"Nothing about me is permanent," he said, "and I think nothing about you is, either."

She blinked. She'd left home and moved to Lonely Hearts Station, the next town over from Union Junction, to be taken in by Delilah Honeycutt, the owner of the Lonely Hearts Salon. When the salon hit a rough patch and Delilah had to lighten up fifty percent of her staff, Lily and the other ladies had come to Union Junction—at the behest of the Jefferson brothers of Malfunction Junction ranch—to start over. It was arranged that Lily would be the manager, and she thought everyone would agree they'd made a successful run of their salon.

But Sam was right. If she hadn't come to a place where her gifts were needed, she would have moved on.

"If you want real independence, I can give you that," he whispered against her ear. "Whether that's financial, or from your family, you could achieve what you want most."

If she did not know that this man was from a decent, honorable family—and that he was cut from the same cloth as she was—there was no way she would even consider his offer. She closed her eyes, lulled by his hands and his voice and his promise. "For the price of a marriage certificate," she said.

"It sounds simple, but it's not, Lily," he said. "Peace of mind for my parents, because they'll believe I've settled down, which, remember, they think will make me a happier man. They live out their days on the ranch, assuming I'm going to take it over, which may sound as if I'm being dishonest with them, but I'm not.

"I simply don't know whether or not my younger brother, Phin, might be the better person to do that. We both need more time to figure out a plan. With an arranged marriage, I get simplicity, because you and I have needs that lie along a similar course. And I would get a deep sense of satisfaction that my folks never found it necessary to sell to the Bartholomews.

"Even if we put the ranch up for auction, that family would

find a way to be high bidder. They would utilize an anonymous proxy if we said we didn't want to sell to them." He laughed, but the sound was empty. "They have ways of getting everything they want. Maybe I shouldn't care whether or not they own my family's ranch, but I remember Mr. Bartholomew coming to my dad with his first offer."

She felt Sam's muscles tense at the memory as he continued. "He said, 'Name your price.' My father said he didn't have a price. And Mr. Bartholomew said that one day, he would." Sam laid his head next to Lily's and put an arm over her waist to tuck her up against him. "I never forgot that confident arrogance, and how much it upset my father to have that two-tailed rattler on his property."

Lily's heart sank. She believed her father had said those words; she'd heard him say similar things to other people. And it was true that he always got what he wanted. He said he had plenty of time to wait out other people's misfortune. Her mother wasn't interested in how their lifestyle was achieved. She did care that she always had pretty clothes and an expensive car, and that women in the town sucked up to her—mostly out of fear, Lily had always thought.

Most of all, her mother cared that Lily make a prestigious marriage that would illuminate the Bartholomew name. "I always thought marriage should be between two people who loved each other," Lily said, "but I never wanted to fall in love."

"So we're perfect for each other," Sam said, rolling over to lie slightly on top of her. He gazed down into her eyes. A lock of hair fell over his forehead and Lily thought, "Trim that," and then instantly she censored herself.

She didn't want to change a thing about Sam. He was offering her what she had always wanted.

Freedom.

"There is one more small thing," Sam said.

She waited. "How small?"

"Maybe seven, eight pounds."

She sat up to look at him. "A baby?"

He crossed his arms behind his head and very casually, he nodded. "Could we work that into the agreement?"

Independence of all kinds was her objective, but a baby of her own…that had always been her wildest dream. One she'd never thought she'd have, until now.

"I realize a baby and independence may be at cross purposes," Sam said, "but we could—"

"A baby isn't an ankle weight I'm worried about," Lily interrupted. She took a deep breath. "Sam, you have yourself a bride."

Chapter Three

"Great," Sam said, watching as his new fiancée jumped up from the blanket, shooing her dog off of it. "Are we going somewhere?"

"You're either taking me home or to a wedding chapel," she replied. "Your choice."

He laughed. "Only place we can strike our bargain in total anonymity is Las Vegas. I have my truck gassed up, if you're of a mind to travel."

"Flying's faster. And I like the anonymity you're suggesting. Vegas sounds like a practical choice. Any other details?"

"Do you need a dress?" he asked.

"No. This is an arranged marriage. No need to buy a white gown for that."

"Hey," Sam said, somehow uncomfortable with her comment. She was right, on the surface. Why did he want her to feel sentimental about a neon-sign-lit wedding?

"Almost too perfect," he said, watching her pack her dog and the blanket neatly into the truck. Samson was so tired he had to be coaxed to jump onto the gate. "Lily," Sam called.

"Yes?"

"Sex before or after the wedding?"

She turned to look at him. He'd seen that look in her eyes

from the moment he'd walked into her salon. "Before, during and after, if you like."

She was too perfect! "Maybe I should test you on that," he said, "after all, I really don't know you. Maybe you're not a girl of your word."

She lifted a brow. "Maybe you haven't given me an engagement ring yet, cowboy."

Ah. Sly and practical. He liked that.

She pulled off her top, and he liked that even better. "Whoa," he said.

"Stop?" Lily asked, looking disappointed.

"Definitely not that kind of whoa," Sam said, "and let that be the last misunderstanding we ever have. Come here, you." He grabbed her, holding her tight to him and undoing her jeans with one hand. "I can't believe you're so gorgeous and you're going to be mine."

He couldn't stop kissing her, and she couldn't seem to stop kissing him back, hurriedly undoing his jeans. His breath seemed to stop when he felt the warmth between her legs. It was just too much goodness and pleasure, and he hadn't felt that in a long time. Lifting her onto him, he leaned against the truck bed, completely stiffening when she slid onto him as if she was made for him.

"Oh, Sam," she said, her arms wrapped tightly around his neck.

He could feel her bare breasts against his chest and he told himself next time they were going to take it slow. But right now, he wanted to rebel-yell his pleasure to the sky.

When she put her feet against the truck gate and pushed herself back and forth along him, he thought he was going to die. He moved one hand to caress her, giving him great satisfaction that they'd slowed down long enough for him to please her.

He buried his face between her breasts, and when she moaned, then tightened on him, Sam grabbed her fanny in both hands, greedily pulling her tightly against him until she cried out.

Her pleasure brought him to climax, and the best feeling he thought he'd ever had was her tightly holding him, every part of her body melded to his.

She was too perfect. She was the woman every man dreamed of.

But she had only agreed to be his so she could be free.

"You're quite a man, fiancé," Lily said, kissing his neck and then his mouth. He closed his eyes, enjoying her touch, but his heart beat a worried tattoo.

What if he accidentally did the unthinkable—and fell in love with a woman who didn't even want a real wedding gown?

"Let's do it again," she murmured against his neck. "Do you want to?"

Perfection obviously had its price—but she was clearly a woman of her word. "Yes," he said, beginning to enjoy the parts of her he'd missed the first time.

THEY LEFT SAMSON WITH HIS favorite "baby-sitters," the other ladies at the salon, and hit the road the next day. By the time they arrived in Las Vegas, Lily was sure of one thing: she loved the way Sam made her body sing.

They'd made love in her room while she packed. They enjoyed a quickie on a pit stop at the airport, and though Lily had giggled through the entire incident, Sam hadn't seemed to mind. When she suggested that it was her opinion that sex in an airplane lavatory was probably highly overrated but perhaps they should check it out and see, Sam laughed so loud that passengers turned to stare.

The problem was, it wasn't just her body that Sam made sing. He was a really good man. Generous, fun, sexy. Everything a woman wanted. He wanted to marry her, and he wanted them to have a child.

She felt as if her fairy godmother had arrived with a giant wand, waving it capriciously over her life.

Was love at first sight possible? Could she be so fortunate?

Sam's hand closed over hers in a completely kind, caring gesture as they stood outside the chapel. She wore a pretty white summer dress, and he wore a black jacket and blue jeans with a western hat and a silver-tipped bolo. If her prince had arrived to coincide with the capricious fairy godmother, she didn't want to mess this up.

And yet she was having a hard time admitting to him her connection to the Bartholomews.

From living with her parents, she knew that lies did not a healthy marriage make. But it was more than that. Sam *deserved* the truth. It was his dream she was trying to fulfill, as well as her own, Lily reminded herself, and the decent thing to do was tell him who her family was.

He would, of course, not marry her. There would be no continued glorious adventure together, no marriage of independence, no child.

"What was I thinking?" Lily murmured.

Sam scooped her up and carried her inside the chapel. "You weren't, and neither was I. Don't get cold feet on me now, bride. You're all mine. I was lucky enough to find you, and I'm keeping you."

She nuzzled against his neck, inhaling his scent and enjoying his strength. It felt great to be in Sam's arms.

"Hello," a kindly elderly woman greeted them, coming forward to welcome them to the chapel. "Welcome to Wedding Dreams."

"Oh, gosh," Lily murmured. "This *is* a dream."

"We'd like to get married," Sam said.

"Sam—" Lily said.

"We'd be delighted to make your dreams come true," the woman said. "I'm Mrs. MacIntosh. My husband is Pastor

MacIntosh. I will be your witness today, and we're so pleased to be able to preside at your very romantic wedding."

Lily clutched Sam's arm. "Sam—"

"Your very best package," Sam said, "but please don't take too long. My bride and I are in a hurry."

A case of nerves hit Lily.

"If you'll just sign in," Mrs. MacIntosh said. "And let's get the tedious business of payment out of the way while Pastor gets dressed. Also, I'll need your marriage license."

"Oh. We'll need to get that," Sam said.

"Then if you just walk down the street, you will find the courthouse." Mrs. MacIntosh beamed. "Come right back here, and we'll be waiting for you."

"Come on, bride," Sam said.

"All right, cowboy." Good! This would give her a chance to tell Sam the truth. She gave Mrs. MacIntosh a weak smile and let Sam lead her away.

On the walk to the courthouse, she formulated her plan. "Sam, I need to tell you something."

"Great. But let's do this quickly. The posted hours show that they close soon." He grinned down at her. "Besides, I'm in a hurry to be honeymooning."

He opened the door and they went inside.

A smiling woman who looked like Lily's grandmother took one look at Lily's eyelet sheath and pushed a marriage certificate onto the table in front of her. "I'll need to see identification, lovebirds," she said. "I can tell you're in a hurry," she teased Sam.

Lily felt herself go weak at the knees.

"Let me have your identification," Sam said.

Lily stared at him, then at the smiling woman.

"Anything will do, dear. Birth certificate, passport, et cetera. My, you look a bit pale, honey."

Sam looked at her. "Lily, are you all right?"

Was she? She wasn't going to be in a moment. She was

going to lose Sam, and there was nothing she could do about that. Not with their family's feud between them.

"Sam, I have to tell you something," she said.

"Good, honey, sign your name right here," the lady said.

There was no help for it. In her large, elegant hand she wrote "Lily Bartholomew" across the paper.

Sam leaned to watch her write. "I feel stupid. I never asked you your whole name...." Perplexed, he looked up at Lily. "Lily Bartholomew?"

She felt her fingers tremble and her eyes water as she clutched her purse. "Yes."

"Not...Lily *Bartholomew*."

He looked so angry. All the kindness and excitement and pleasure she'd seen in his eyes a moment ago had disappeared, to be replaced by cold, compassionless estrangement.

The traveler he'd been before he sat in her stylist's chair returned. "Yes. Lily Bartholomew."

He was silent for a moment. "Do your parents know about me asking you to marry me? Did you tell them, Lily? Does your father think he finally has what he wants?"

"No." She shook her head. "Sam, this is just me. It has nothing to do with my family."

"It has everything to do with your family." He stared at her, then his hand took hold of her wrist. "And mine. Let me pay, and we will take our hard-won marriage certificate up to the romantic chapel so that we can be married."

"But—" Lily was worried about Sam. "You're still marrying me?"

"Most certainly. Thank you," he said to the clerk when she'd handed him the paperwork. He hustled Lily back to the wedding chapel. "You are all my dreams come true, bride."

She didn't believe him for a second. "You're all my dreams come true, too," she said, meaning it.

"I'm glad." He sent her a smile, but it was so cold she didn't dare believe him. Why was he acting like this? She'd expected him to want out, maybe even ditch her in Vegas. No, Sam was too much a gentleman to do that, but she hadn't expected he'd still want to marry her.

They stood in front of Pastor MacIntosh, and the short ceremony was almost a relief. Lily said "I do" and Sam did, too, and Mrs. MacIntosh played some pretty music on the piano that Lily barely heard. Then, with a toss of rose petals from Mrs. MacIntosh, Sam and Lily exited the chapel.

She looked at the lovely diamond ring Sam had placed on her finger, hardly believing it was there. "Sam, I'm scared."

He looked at her. "Well, don't be. We conducted a business deal to which we both agreed. I'll have a lawyer draw up the papers. But you know you stand to lose far more than I do. And I don't want anything you have, so you're safe."

She blinked, feeling her heart shatter. "Now what?"

"Now I go home. My parents will be delighted that I have a bride and am settling down, by their definition. Only you know I have no intention of ever settling down with you."

"What about us?"

"There is no us. I will send you a check periodically to cover the independence of which you dream, in return for staying married to me."

Lily felt tears beginning to prick the back of her eyes. "Why did you marry me?"

He looked at her, his eyes ruthless. "Well, at first I wanted to marry you because I almost thought I was falling in love with you. Everything about you was…" A regretful expression crossed his face. "I should have known you were too good to be true. But now I take great comfort in the fact that your father loses. I guess I can sacrifice a broken heart. The old goat can wait as long as he wants to, and he won't get anything more than a Christmas card from me or my family. The Johnston ranch wins, and I have his daughter."

"Our marriage is a game to you?"

"Hey, you picked the field," he said, "I'm just playing inside the lines." He put his hat on his head and waved down a taxi.

AFTER A SILENT FLIGHT back to Texas, Sam dropped Lily off at the salon. He gave her a thousand dollars that she didn't want to take, but he made her. A bargain was a bargain, after all, and he owed her a lot more for what she was giving him, but it was all the cash he had on him at the moment. Once home, he would have papers drawn up and money transferred to her account.

Perversely, now that he'd decided to spend a little time with his parents to test out the ranching life, something inside him wanted to know that Lily was well taken care of. He wanted her to stay married to him. It wasn't just about keeping his parents' ranch in the family; he really had fallen for her, before he knew she'd deceived him.

He got into his truck and hit the road, heading toward home.

Something else was bothering him, he decided as he drove through Amarillo, a long stretch of yellow land that gave a man time to think. What had Lily really stood to gain by marrying him?

She was in cahoots with her father, and this was a way to please him.

If that was the case, she wouldn't have agreed to a quickie, secret wedding.

Maybe this was a way to get into her family's good graces. She had said she was the black sheep.

Again, she'd made no mention of wanting to tell her family about him, no dragging him before the family like a trophy, no hope that he would ask her father for her hand in marriage.

Which, he figured, he should have done…but when she'd said she was the black sheep, he had figured she wouldn't want that.

How black a sheep could she be, if her father was a Bartholomew? Now, that was a black ram of the meanest lineage.

Lily had proved she wasn't sweet.

She might be opportunistic, though.

The truth was, he didn't know her. He might have been bowled over by her calmness and her gentleness and definitely by the way she made love to him—constantly and everywhere. But sex wasn't everything.

"It's a lot," he said to himself as he watched a hawk glide overhead in the almost-colorless sky. Just thinking about making love to Lily made his horses run.

But it didn't matter. She was who she was and he was who he was—and the two of them should have never met in the first place.

Chapter Four

Two months after her incredible, whirlwind marriage to Sam, Lily took herself to Doc to complain of summertime flu.

Doc laughed at her. "Not flu," he said. "Congratulations. You're going to have a baby." He grinned widely. "Those are my favorite words to say."

She stared at him. "A baby?"

Sam's baby?

Her heart skipped a beat, but she couldn't tell if it was from excitement or dread. She was excited to be pregnant, especially with his baby. Yet there was no way he'd be happy about it. She hadn't heard from him since he'd left. A generous monthly allotment was deposited to her bank account. He'd had her lawyers send her paperwork abolishing all claim either of them had on the other financially. She'd signed the papers and sent them back quickly, not caring about the postnuptial agreement.

But this postnuptial surprise was a biggie. "You're sure?"

"I've been a country doctor a long time. I'm sure." He wrote an address on a piece of paper for her. "I need you to make an appointment with this medical group. I want you to go in and have a sonogram and take whatever tests they deem necessary."

Lily shook her head. "Your sonogram was fine. I'd rather you handle my pregnancy matters."

"Well, there's just a small thing I want the city boys to

check out. These are friends of mine, and if what I'm guessing is correct, we're going to need them."

"Is there a problem?" Lily asked, her heart beating hard.

Doc grinned. "I think you're going to be a very happy lady."

TWO WEEKS LATER, WHEN Lily was finally able to get in for the additional sonogram, she felt like a watermelon was lodged in her stomach, and she was irritable.

She wasn't ready to tell Sam, but she was scared of being pregnant alone. And she didn't know how to tell him that he was going to be a father. He had wanted a child—until he found out it would have Bartholomew blood.

"Well, well," the city doc said. "Four little Texas babies. Better put a long distance call into…where did you say? Montana?"

Lily blinked, her heart slowing at the same time a sense of panic set in. "Four?"

He grinned. "Four. And they look healthy. You're mighty lucky. If you were in Vegas, we'd call this hitting the jackpot."

Lily didn't smile. "I was married in Vegas," she said dully.

"There you have it. Good luck must have rubbed off on you."

"I don't think so," Lily said quietly, gathering her purse and standing to leave his office. "But thank you."

She returned to the salon, running straight to her room to have a good, frightened cry. How could she be pregnant with four children? It was beyond her wildest imaginings.

When she didn't leave her room for two days, Delilah came looking for her. "Hey, honey," Delilah said. "It's not all that bad, is it? This is not like you, Lily."

"I know." Lily sat up against the pillows. "I used to be so strong. I was always so proud of my independence. Now all I do is lie here and cry into Samson's fur."

Delilah laughed. "Maybe you'd feel better if you called your husband."

"No." Lily shook her head. "I can't. I'm in shock. I never

really knew what that meant before, but now I completely understand what people meant when they said they were in shock." She blew into the tissue Delilah handed her. "Do you remember when the great storm hit Malfunction Junction? The Jefferson men told us they were in shock when they asked for our help, but it just seemed like time to knuckle down and do some work to me."

"Of course, back then this town wasn't our home yet," Delilah murmured.

"Well, what did you do when Valentine burned down your kitchen and part of your salon? How did you go on?"

Delilah laughed. "To be honest, I may have felt a few hours of shock, but I felt sorrier for Valentine than anything. The worst thing that ever happened to me was when my sister, Marvella, accused me of trying to steal her husband. Now, I did feel shock then. And for many years, every time I thought about it, my stomach turned." Delilah shook her head. "That's the only way I can describe it, and that doesn't even do the feeling justice."

"I feel sick," Lily said. "I don't know Sam well enough to have four children by him!" She started to cry again, big, fat tears running down her cheeks. "People who have been married for six or seven years can get used to the idea of four children, arriving one at a time. But this stork's going to have to bring in the double-wide to get them all here—oh, my gosh!" She looked up at Delilah, feeling stunned. "Where am I going to put four babies?"

Delilah sighed. "I think you'll have to move."

Of course she would. She'd have to leave her room above the salon, the only home where she'd really been happy, besides Delilah's in Lonely Hearts Station. She would be more alone than ever, because she wouldn't have her stylist sisters in the house with her. It was like one giant dormitory, with all of them sharing their lives.

"I don't know what I'm going to do," she murmured. "I'm going to be the mother to four little people."

"And you'll be fine. You're so responsible, Lily. You always have been the most levelheaded of the girls."

"Obviously not," Lily said, "or I wouldn't have gotten swept off my feet by Sam."

"You must have liked his brand of broom," Delilah said, with a sly wink. "Think about calling him, honey. Pregnancy is a restart button in people's lives. It changes everything."

"I know," Lily said. But he had left her. She wasn't about to call a man who didn't want her.

Delilah left the room, and Lily sat in the dim light, pondering her multitude of blessings.

FALL CAME, AND SAM refused to allow himself to think about Lily, though his parents asked often why they couldn't meet his new bride.

"She's working," he said. "You'll meet her soon enough. Be happy that everything worked out the way it did."

Old man Bartholomew had been hopping mad that Sam's folks had refused his offer. Secretly married to Lily, Sam had enjoyed his frustration all the more.

Except he missed her. Terribly.

"You don't belong here," Phin said on one of his trips home. "Why are you suddenly working yourself to death on the ranch?"

Sam gave him a sidelong glance. "I'm tired of rodeo and traveling. Time to settle down."

"I don't think so," Phin said. "I'm settling somewhere else."

"Then be glad I'm willing to stay here."

"Yeah." Phin scratched his head. "I'm looking at two plans. One for a golf course, and one for a ski lodge. I can't decide which of my favorite pastimes to pursue."

Sam had gone after Lily and lost, so what did he know about pursuits? "Can't help you, bro. Sorry."

"So what's with the secrecy act about your wedding? Do you really have a wife?"

"Yeah. I do." Sam tossed a saddle over a gate and looked out across a wide endless field. It really was pretty here. But it would be prettier if he had Lily in this field with him. "I'm an idiot," Sam said.

"Sometimes," Phin agreed, "but aren't we all?"

Sam put his boot on the rail fence and took off his hat. "I guess. Anyway, do both."

"Both?"

"Both of your pursuits. Can't you run a system where you have a ski lodge in the winter, then in the summer, when there's no snow, run a golf course?"

Phin blinked. "A year-round tourist attraction."

"Yeah. Maybe for honeymooners."

"Honeymooners," Phin said slowly. "It's so crazy it might work. I'll have to look before I leap. I don't like lack of planning, as you know."

"Lack of planning got me a wife," Sam said.

"I was going to ask you about that," Phin said. "I wouldn't do that again, if I were you."

"No, I'm keeping the bride I've got."

"I meant the lack of planning. I plan everything. For example, I don't plan to take over this ranch, ever. Careful planning makes a man's life simple. Happy. Even harmonious. Of course, I always looked up to you as the model of control and good judgment."

"I married Mr. Bartholomew's daughter," Sam said.

Phin stared at him. He blinked owlishly. "Brother, have you lost your mind?"

"Yes. I did." Sam straightened. "Maybe it was a mid-life crisis. Or too long in the Texas heat."

"And maybe a roaming band of gypsies carried off your brain," Phin said. "Mom and Dad are going to put a boot up your—"

Sam held up a hand. "Don't think I haven't kicked myself plenty."

"She must have been plenty hot to get under your skin like that."

"I didn't know who she was. And even though I do now, she makes me smile every time I think about her."

Phin looked at his brother closely. "Oh, man. I should be congratulating you, and all I can think to say is 'I am so sorry.'"

Sam grimaced. "Lack of planning put my neck in a noose. As I say, I can't offer you any advice."

His brother raised his brows. "Sure did make Mom and Dad happy that you'd married. They can't wait to meet her. Don't know how much longer you can hold them off."

"I can't call her," Sam said. "I said terrible things to her when she told me who she was. I was a jerk. I'm still a jerk. I don't know that I can face her, because I want her to be who I thought she was, and not who she is."

"Who did you think she was?"

"The most fabulous, hottest woman I'd ever met," Sam said.

Phin grinned. "You realize Mr. Bartholomew's gonna string you up when he finds out he's related to you."

"To us," Sam said. "You're in this, too."

"Yeah, but I'm going to be off with my tourist-honeymoon attraction," Phin said, "and you're going to be here alone." He frowned. "You know, we just saw the old man yesterday. He was as big a jerk as ever."

"Yeah." Sam could easily agree with that.

"But he didn't know."

Sam looked up. "About what?"

"That you two outlaws were now in-laws."

"So?"

"It means Lily hasn't told him."

Sam shrugged. "What does that mean?"

"It means, goofball, that Lily isn't using you for anything. She doesn't even talk to her parents about you. I mean, every woman blabs to her parents, don't they? Especially her mother."

Sam looked at Phin.

"But she hasn't. Whatever happened between the two of you, stayed between the two of you. She could have used your marriage to help her father, but she didn't. She didn't even tell him, so she's not interested in giving him any ammunition." Phin looked pleased. "This girl could be even hotter than you think she is."

Sam blinked. "I never thought of it that way."

Phin slapped him on the back. "You sure have a funny way of showing appreciation for a good wife. Hope she doesn't decide to run off on you."

He was hit with a spear of jealousy. "She wouldn't."

Phin grinned. "Hot, awesome women are hard to find. They're nearly as impossible as an eight-second bull ride scoring over ninety."

That was true, too. Sam fought off the sinking feeling in his stomach. "I've got to get back to work."

"Just food for thought," Phin said cheerfully. "Seems like you've been missing the dessert course."

"Very funny," Sam said, but Phin's words stayed with him as he rode up to the house and went inside. On the kitchen table was a couriered letter, addressed to him, from someone he didn't know. Curious, he pulled it open.

Dear Mr. Johnston,
There's something in Union Junction, Texas, that requires your urgent attention.

It wasn't signed. Slow, deep pounding developed inside Sam's head. The letter could only refer to Lily. He should call and check on her.

That would put his mind to rest on many issues. Going to his room, he sat down on the bed and dialed information for the salon's phone number. A few moments later, he asked for Lily's room, and was connected.

He wondered if she'd be home. He wondered if she'd hang up on him.

"Hello?" Lily said.

"Lily, it's Sam." Surely she could hear the booming of his heart.

"Hello, Sam."

He was so relieved she didn't slam the phone down in his ear. "How are you doing?"

"I'm…fine," she said. "You?"

"Couldn't be better." It was a lie, but he had to save face.

"Are you calling to say you want a divorce?" Lily asked.

"Hell, no," he said. "Why would I?"

"I don't know. Why would you want to stay married?" Lily held her breath, rubbing her extended belly as she waited for Sam's answer.

Chapter Five

"We had an agreement," he finally said. "I'm good for my end."

That wasn't what she wanted to hear, but it was going to have to be enough for now.

"I saw your father the other day," Sam said.

"Oh." She had been thinking about her father lately, wondering how he would feel if he knew he was going to be a grandfather.

"He was pretty sore that we had decided not to sell to him."

"He'll get over it," she said. "Do you know that Christmas is in a few weeks?"

"I haven't given Christmas much thought."

"I have," she said softly. "Do you think married people should spend Christmas together?"

"Haven't thought much about that, either," Sam said. "But I suppose you're right."

"I've got a special gift for you for Christmas," Lily said. "I hope you'll like it."

"You're an early shopper."

This year, she'd have to be. "I'm going to move, Sam. Just so you'll know."

"Move?"

"Yes. I'm looking for a bigger place."

"I thought you liked living at the salon."

"I do. I love it. But it's time for me to move on."

"Do you need help?"

She was surprised by his offer. "That's all right. I know you're busy with the ranch, and fall is a busy time."

"Lily, if you need help with something, all you have to do is call."

"I think...I need help," she said slowly.

"Name it."

She took a deep breath. "I need to know if what we had was real."

He was silent for a long time. "I don't know myself."

"Have you forgiven me yet?"

"Lily, I don't know if *forgiveness* is the right word. It's impossible. Even if what we had was real, it's impossible."

Her heart seemed to fall to pieces, bit by bit.

"I'm not mad," he said, "and the past is in the past. Even where your father is concerned. I'm done with all of that. Marrying you gave me the freedom to forget about him."

"Marrying you gave me the power to remember him," she said. "Goodbye, Sam."

Quietly, she hung up the phone.

It was true. Besides the babies, the important thing that had come into her heart was forgiveness for her family's ways.

TEN HOURS LATER—ALMOST TO the minute—Lily heard an authoritative knock on her door. Samson sat up on her bed, his ears perked. Opening the door, she was shocked to find Sam standing outside, holding a giant bouquet of flowers.

"Hi," she said.

"Hello," he replied. Then his gaze fell to her overlarge belly. *"Hello."*

Lily closed the door behind him. "What brings you here?"

"Your theory of forgiveness. Only now I'm mad again."

She sighed. "I know. I can feel your blood pressure shooting up about a thousand points."

"Why didn't you tell me?"

Lily sat on the bed. "I wanted to. But there was nothing between us that was permanent."

"Just *marriage*."

"Never once did you indicate any further interest in me after you left," she pointed out.

"So, being the independent woman you are, you decided to be a single parent."

She shrugged. "I felt I had no choice."

He scratched his head. "I don't know what to say."

"You said everything necessary on the phone last night. You said it was impossible."

"That's before I knew there was a baby!"

He was so handsome, Lily thought, even more than she had remembered. By contrast, she felt overwhelmingly pushed out of shape. "It's been such a surprise," she said. "I know that's not a good excuse, but I had a lot to work through with my family."

"Do they know?"

She shook her head. "They don't even know I'm married."

"So what did you work through?"

"Forgiveness." She gave him a level gaze. "I had to. Babies make you realize that nothing matters except them."

He sat down next to her. "Now what?"

"Tomorrow I move into my new house. After that, I'm on bed rest."

"You look beautiful."

She smiled. "Thank you."

"Someone sent me an anonymous note saying that you needed me. Now I see just how much."

She shook her head. "I don't need you."

"Yes, you do." He nodded. "You need your husband."

"You're not really a husband. We have no future."

"No," Sam said, "we were living in the past. But now we've both changed. We're growing. And now we're going to grow together and live in the future. I'm going to live here in Union Junction with you, where your doctors are, until you're ready to move to Montana with me."

"I hardly know what to say."

"Say yes," he told her. "You're going to need a friend."

"Actually," Lily said, getting up, "you probably need a friend more than me."

"I've got Phin. He's not really a friend, but he's excellent backup."

Lily took a deep breath. "I have a little confession to make."

"One thing I've already learned about you is that you are a woman of secrets. How little is little, anyway?"

"About twelve to fifteen pounds," Lily said.

His eyes widened. "You're expecting a fifteen-pound baby?" He patted Samson, who had laid his head in his lap. "What has your mother been eating, son?"

Lily hesitated. "I don't know how to tell you this."

He quit patting Samson to stare at her. "I've never seen you this worried, not even when you told me who your family was. This must be a doozy."

"We're having quadruplets," she said.

He frowned. "Four babies?"

"Yes."

He didn't move. He simply sat and stared at her. She couldn't read the expression in his dark brown eyes.

Finally, she realized he was in shock. "Sam?" she said softly.

"You are the most amazing woman I've ever met," Sam said. "I don't know if I can handle you."

She laughed nervously. "Are you going to be okay with this?"

"Yes," he said. "But you get your father on the phone, and you tell him to get down here right now. Says Sam Johnston of Falling Hills Ranch. Your *husband*."

"Sam—"

"That's it from now on," Sam said as he pulled her next to him in the bed. "You can't keep a single secret from me. You nearly gave me a heart attack!" He felt his chest, surprised his heart hadn't jumped out of it, then curled up behind Lily, deciding that this was worth the agony. "I have never slept the whole night with you in bed."

"Maybe you shouldn't now," Lily said.

"I'm not spending one more night apart from you," Sam said, "especially now that I've seen you in your granny gown."

"If I'd known you were coming, I would have bought something more appropriate," she said crossly.

"No, you wouldn't have, unless it was a suit of armor. The element of surprise seems to work very well with you. I like the granny gown, holes and all."

"There are no holes!"

He moved his erection against her backside. "I wish there were."

Lily sat up. "Sam. I probably can't have sex for another, like, millennium. I don't even know how I'm going to bring four babies into this world. You're making me nervous!"

"Sh," he said. "Lie on your side and let me rub your back. Good thing we had a lot while we could."

Lily sighed. "Remember when we talked about having a child?"

"All I know is that we have to start over, from the beginning, and restart the dream clock," Sam said. "You're a sneaky girl."

"Sneaky!"

He rubbed her back, then slipped his hand around to hold her stomach. "I get five for the price of one. Helluva deal. My dad's going to be impressed."

"My father's going to be chapped," Lily said.

"Well, the holidays will be interesting," Sam said. "Think

of our two fathers sitting at a table together, eating cranberry sauce and pumpkin pie and cussing each other."

Lily giggled.

"When were you going to tell me?" Sam asked, still struggling with sudden fatherhood.

"Never," Lily said, her voice sleepy. "You're an arrogant big thing. And I didn't like you."

"But I'll be a great dad," Sam told her. "You're a lucky girl. I rub feet and other things," he said, reaching down to caress her bottom. "So, we're moving tomorrow?"

"I am moving tomorrow," Lily said. "You are not coming with me."

"Yes, I am. Samson and me are a package deal."

"I am going to have to let Samson be adopted," Lily said sadly.

"Why?" He could feel the dog lying on his feet—it didn't seem fair to kick the canine to the floor just yet—and it was oddly comforting.

"Sam, four babies are going to preclude pets. I'm just hoping I can get them all fed and diapered every couple of hours."

"Oh," Sam said. "I see. I'll feed the dog."

Lily rolled over to face him. "You don't understand. It's not that easy."

"Sure it is. I feed cattle. I can feed a dog."

"You're not going to be around."

He rolled her over to face him, giving her a deep kiss. "Just try and get rid of me," he said.

Chapter Six

There was one overriding thing bothering Sam. "While I may not let you run me off," Sam told Lily, "I don't trust you. No more secrets. The first two have been huge, and I swear I'm aging."

"No more secrets," Lily assured him. "Everything is out in the open."

"Good," he said, cupping her breast with one hand. "Marriage should be an open door."

Lily laughed. "You mean an open book."

"Whatever." He nuzzled her neck and then her breast. "You can leave the door open, but I'm hanging around for more of this."

Lily's hand moved to a very auspicious part of his body, and Sam felt himself paying very close attention to what she was doing. "And more of that," he said.

She giggled, and Sam held her tighter, enjoying her. A few moments later, she reached her goal of pleasuring him, and Sam sighed deeply against Lily's hair.

If this was marriage, he could handle it.

IF THIS WAS MARRIAGE, Lily wasn't certain she could handle it.

Sam was too nice to her. Too understanding. Too perfect.

She was going to fall in love with him. Or maybe she was

already in love. She patted her stomach, looking at the large protrusion that, somehow, miraculously held four babies. It was completely beyond her understanding.

Sam sat up in the bed, rubbing his hair with one sleepy hand. "Hey, beautiful. Can't sleep?"

"I'm an early riser."

He frowned. "You don't have to work today, do you?"

She looked at him, and at the dawn light coming through her eyelet curtains, and wished she could know whether they could be happy together forever. Did the bond of parenthood forge a happy relationship?

"I don't have to work. It's moving day, remember?"

He hopped out of bed—naked—and Lily blinked. "Okay, only one of us in this room is beautiful right now, and it's not me."

Grinning, he swept her up in his arms, lying her back in the bed. He covered her up to her chin with a sheet. "You stay in bed. Let me take care of everything, beautiful."

"I can't, Sam. It's moving day!"

"You only get to do what I say." He winked at her. "I'm going to take a shower, and I want you to lie in that bed and not move, little mama. And then we're going to talk about our new house. Samson, hop up here," he said, and the dog dutifully obeyed. "Your mother thinks she can't feed you and so she's threatening not to take you with her, but she didn't realize she was packing me on moving day, too. Lie right here and make sure she doesn't go anywhere."

Samson rolled on his back, wanting to be patted. Lily shrugged at Sam. "He doesn't mind very well."

"Well, he gets his independent streak from his mother. Stay in bed, and let me take care of you. I'm just certain that carrying boxes isn't what the doctor would recommend."

"But no one knows where I want things to go."

"I'll figure it out." He grabbed some pants from his duffel

bag. "I know that dishes go in a kitchen, and baby things go in a nursery, and so on."

"Okay, but I'm coming with you," Lily said, getting out of the bed. "Sam, I won't touch a box, I promise. But I have to oversee the move-in to my own house!"

He grinned. "All right. You can come with me," he said, dragging her into the bathroom with him. Pulling her gown over her head, he flipped on the shower water to warm. "The only hard work I want you to do is this," he said, holding her close to him as they got under the water. Then he stood close to her, holding her, his head against hers while he stroked her bottom. They stood like that for a long time, being together, and Lily closed her eyes, wishing she wasn't starting to feel so scared.

Never in her life had anything felt so good.

So unbelievably right.

DELILAH AND HER BOYFRIEND, Jerry, came over to help Lily move, as had Mason and Last Jefferson from the Malfunction Junction ranch. Lily had known the Jefferson brothers since she'd first come out to Union Junction, and they were like big brothers to her.

Only Sam didn't seem to understand that two handsome cowboys hanging around his wife was a good thing. He was unusually quiet. "Are you all right?" she asked Sam when he'd finished loading her things into the back of Jerry's long-haul truck.

"I'm fine."

"You seem out of sorts," Lily said.

He shrugged. "I said I'm fine."

Mason and Last came around the truck, stuffing some moving blankets over the items most likely to shift on the way over to the new house. "That's it," Mason said. "Told you it wouldn't take long with all this manpower." He gave Sam a hearty slap on the back. "You didn't have to bring along a husband to help you, Lily. We Jeffersons will always take care of you."

Last nodded, giving her a brotherly kiss on the cheek. "All right," he said. "Off we go to your new house."

Jerry started up the truck and Delilah got in the front seat. Mason and Last jumped in their truck. Sam stared at Lily, his forehead creased.

"What?" Lily said.

"They seem awfully close to you," Sam said.

"We're friends." Her worried gaze searched his face. "Nothing romantic?"

"As in, did I ever date one of them?" Lily asked. "No. Why would you ask?"

"Because I could have moved you myself. It wasn't like you had that much stuff. Seems like it's my job to do."

"But you weren't here," Lily pointed out.

"But I would have been, if you'd been honest." Sam shook his head. "It'll wear off." He began walking toward his truck.

Lily followed after him. "What will wear off?"

"The jealousy. I'm sure that's all it is. I'm suffering from normal feelings that any man in my position would feel at finding two large, rangy, tough cowboys moving his wife's possessions."

Lily smiled, catching Sam's arm. "Sam, you are not jealous when I'm so fat and hugely stuffed out of shape, and about to go on complete bed rest?"

Sam kissed her hard, possessively. "I think you're in my blood," he said when he pulled away. "In the wild, the lion who intends to have the lioness kills off his younger, weaker rivals."

Lily laughed. "Sam, the Jefferson brothers are not rivals. They're like my big brothers. So don't kill them off, please. Mason's in love with Mimi Cannady—has been for years. And Last has a young daughter to raise." She stroked his face, realizing for the first time the power of the sexual attraction between them. "I've never known anyone like you."

"I sort of like your mystery and your sass, as much as I worry that you might use that confession against me."

Lily gave him a sweet smile. "To set the record straight, I don't think Mason or Last are either weaker or necessarily younger."

"Lily," Sam said on a growl.

Lily laughed, kissed him on the mouth and got into the truck. She looked out the open window at him. "Come on, cowboy. I'm looking forward to decorating my house for Christmas."

"Our house." Sam whistled, and Samson came running to hop in the truck, seating himself happily next to Lily. Sam got in, starting the engine. "He's been lurking around, trying to figure out what was going on. Both of us were afraid you were going to try to leave us behind."

Lily shook her head. "You have both shown that you won't be left."

"And on that subject," Sam said, "I'll be needing to make house payments for us."

"No," Lily said. "You've done enough. With the money you've sent, I was able to buy a home."

"Yes, and you've more than kept up your part of the bargain. In fact, you quadrupled our original agreement. Further, I called your father last night."

Lily gasped, but Sam just calmly followed the Jeffersons' truck, which was behind Jerry's hauler, onto the highway.

"For a lot of reasons, we've started this marriage out covertly. If it's going to last, we need to put things right. Which means, I need to ask your father for your hand in marriage."

"We're already married!"

"Yes." Sam looked thoughtful. "But that was in a chapel in Las Vegas with neon lights, and no parents in attendance.

I'm suggesting we have a Christmas ceremony for our parents' sake, our children's sake, and most of all, our sake."

Lily shook her head. "Sam, I'm big as a house. I don't want to get married while I look like this."

"You are the most beautiful woman I have ever seen," Sam said simply. "But we need to do this right, without an agreement binding us."

"Marriage is an agreement," Lily pointed out.

"Yes, but we had the agreement and then the wedding."

"And then the separation," Lily reminded him.

"Precisely. This time, we're going to do the wedding and then all the agreements. Which way the toilet paper roll goes, who gets the TV remote…" He was silent for a moment.

"Your father was very surprised to hear from me," Sam continued. "I hope you don't mind that I invited him down here. It's too far for you to travel to go back home, so this is easier for you."

Lily blinked. "You invited my parents for Christmas?"

"Yes."

"How did Dad take hearing from you?"

"He seemed happy, until I told him that his visit would concern his daughter." Sam grinned. "Then I believe I heard a foul word questioning my heritage come out of his mouth."

"Oh." Lily's heart sank.

"Remember when you said that you wanted independence?"

"Yes," Lily murmured.

"Marrying me will do it," Sam said cheerfully. "I could hear it in your father's tone. He does not like me at all, and the feeling's mutual."

"Sam?"

"Yes, bride?" He patted her hand, and Samson licked his face.

"I have two tiny little things to tell you."

Sam stopped the truck. "How tiny? A fifth baby would be very tiny," he said.

"No, it's not about that," Lily said. "It's about your Christmas present." She took a deep breath. "Since you said you were staying here with me, and the babies will have arrived by then, I knew your parents and brother would probably miss you. So, for your Christmas gift, I invited them to share the holidays with us."

"Oops." Sam shrugged. "Well, Samson will get lots of scraps from all the food that gets left on everyone's plates as they rush out the door."

"Are you mad?"

"No," Sam said, "we'll assign each of them a baby for diaper duty, and I'm going to spend Christmas in bed with my wife. Wear a bow for me to unwrap."

"About that…the second thing is—" Lily took a deep breath "—Sam, I don't want to marry you again."

Chapter Seven

Sam parked behind the Jefferson brothers' truck before he replied to Lily's statement. There was a Lily's House sign stretched across the front porch of a dilapidated schoolhouse, which looked to be no more than one room.

Very small.

A mailbox had been put in the front yard, and there were about twenty women out front, stringing Christmas lights in the bushes. There was a white rocker on the front porch, and a wreath on the front door.

"You do want to marry me," he said, not entirely convinced now. The house looked tiny, and not the rambling ranch house he was used to. "We need to do everything right, the way it should be."

"No," Lily said softly. "I'm sorry, Sam, but I don't think another wedding is in our future."

"I don't understand you, woman," Sam said, not wanting to talk any more about it right now, not until he could get his emotions under control. "Did you know that our new house appears to be a previous house of academia?"

Lily smiled. "Is it not the most darling thing you've ever seen?"

Sam hesitated. "Well, if I'd been an enthusiastic student—"

"The Jeffersons are developing plans to build on a second

floor," Lily said. "I thought it was a good idea. And it's close to the animal rescue shelter the Union Junction stylists started."

"So this is your dream home?" Sam was trying to see himself living in a school and failing miserably. "I made A's in school, but never saw myself living with a chalkboard in my living room."

Lily looked at him. "You left," she reminded him. "I had to make practical choices. I was able to purchase the surrounding ten acres from the owner of the next house. So our children will have lots of room to run and play."

"So you picked out a house," Sam said, "and made renovation plans, but never thought about calling me to tell me I was going to be a father?"

All of a sudden, a whole bunch of confusing emotions poured through his body. He wanted them to stop—now—but he couldn't seem to make them. Looking at the house, he came to a stark realization: Once he'd left, Lily had never planned for him to be part of her life. And now she didn't want to marry him again.

Mason opened the door. "You two getting out?"

Sam stepped out as Samson rushed past him, while Last helped Lily slowly get out of the truck.

"She won't marry me," Sam said, more to himself than Mason, but it came out aloud, anyway.

"Oh. I'm no help with that," Mason said. "Women trouble is my middle name. And there's no use in asking Last, because—"

"Hey!" Last glared at his older brother. "I'm getting mine figured out."

Lily looked at him. "It's just the way I feel, Sam."

She walked into her new house, surrounded by eager ladies who led her inside. Even Samson, that traitor, bounded inside the house with his plumy tail happily waving.

Sam felt very deserted. Unwelcome, even.

"Women," Mason said. "They have minds of their own, and it's pretty irritating at times."

Sam nodded. "She's made all these plans without me."

"Well." Mason crossed his arms. "You'll just have to take the castle by storm."

Last stared at his big brother. "You are not giving out relationship advice, are you?" He shook his head. "Traveler, I wouldn't listen to anything he says about love, unless you want to live without the only woman you ever loved for your whole life."

Mason pushed his hat down low on his head, then stalked off toward the house. Last followed him, the two of them gesturing at each other as they walked inside the house, the same way Sam and Phin did when they were having a brotherly "meeting of the minds."

That left Sam alone on the pavement. As he saw it, he had two choices: One, he could slink off into the sunset and have a lawyer draw up an arrangement for custodial visitation. Lily liked agreements. She would probably enjoy having a schedule that was predetermined.

Or he could hang on for dear life, as if love was a bounty bull he could ride past the buzzer.

"Phin," he said slowly, "you're going to have to learn to run a ranch by yourself. I've got a schoolhouse to renovate."

"Sam!" Mason waved at him from the front door. "I think you'd better come on in! Quickly!"

Sam jogged up the sidewalk and inside the house. The large room, where desks must once have sat, was fully decorated for Christmas. Garlands ran up a stairwell he hadn't noticed from the front. It was attached at the back of the house—probably leading to a room where the schoolteacher had lived above the school. There was a beautifully lit Christmas tree in the corner, under which four white bassinets lay waiting.

It took his breath away. In short amount of time, those bassinets would be full.

That was all that mattered, he realized. He was going to win Lily's heart no matter what.

"Sam," Lily said.

"Yeah?" Glancing over at her, he noticed her pale color. "Are you all right?"

"I could use a ride to the hospital," she said.

It seemed that the whole room gasped, and then everybody began rushing around, gathering things up and offering to take Lily to the doctor.

"Sam can do it," she told one stylist. "Thank you so much for the lovely housewarming and baby shower."

Urgency penetrated the fog he was in. "Come on, sweetie," he said gently, helping Lily to her feet. "Are we going to have some Christmas angels?"

"I don't know," Lily said. "I feel very strange."

Maybe moving hadn't been such a good idea, Sam thought, guiding Lily to his truck. Then again, where would she have put four babies in a beauty salon? And the schoolhouse had been so charmingly decorated that he knew she'd made a wise and wonderful choice.

He should have been here with Lily, Sam told himself. Then she wouldn't have had to do everything alone. Carefully, he sat her in the truck, then extended the seat belt even farther than it had been. "How can I put this on you so it's not uncomfortable?"

Lily laid her head back against the headrest. "At this point, it doesn't matter. Even my ears suddenly feel swollen."

Sam dashed around to the driver's side of the truck, waving at everyone who was standing on the porch, then drove slowly away. "Okay, Lily, we're on the way. Of course, I have no idea how to get there."

"Head into town," she said quietly. "You'll see Union Junction Hospital after you turn left going opposite of the salon."

"Got it." His mind was shattering into a thousand pieces. Never had he been so scared! And yet so excited.

Lily took little puffing breaths, and Sam felt sweat rim his hat.

"Sam?" Lily said, her voice very feeble.

"Yes?"

She gasped a few more quick breaths. "My father was real hard on us growing up. Very stern. Very by-the-book. His way or the highway."

What was she trying to tell him? He knew her father was a stubborn cuss.

"So another wedding isn't necessary," Lily continued. "It's not going to change the basics of what's between us. We got married because we each needed something. But then we separated because, in not wanting to lose you, I deceived you. And you left, which I can't blame you about. But you came back and you're here now."

She groaned, and Sam wanted to drive faster, his heart racing with fear that something might be wrong. "Lily, let's talk about all this later," Sam said.

"I can't. You have to know why I don't want to marry you again. Dad's stubbornness and my-way attitude eventually drove me away. Don't keep trying to fit us into some ideal of what marriage should be. We didn't start out conventionally, and we're fine the way we are. As far as I'm concerned, I don't need a renewal of vows to put the past behind us. The act of birth, the very beauty of bringing our children into the world, is the marriage to me."

Sam blinked. "Lily, you are so beautiful. I wish we'd been naked together when you said that."

Lily laughed, though it was more a groan than anything. "It's going to be hard, Sam, to be parents. We never got on settled ground as newlyweds."

"I know. But let's not worry about that now." He frowned. "Our house is too small."

"Our? You're really going to stay?"

"Yes," Sam said. "We need another house nearby. You can use the schoolhouse later for homeschooling, if you want, or social gatherings, but you need something big enough to fit me into."

"What about Falling Hills?" Lily asked. "That was the reason we got married!"

"Remember the spiritual wedding we're about to enjoy?" Sam asked. "The one where giving birth restarts our lives together?"

Lily looked at him, her hands surrounding her abdomen protectively. "Yes."

"I'm turning responsibility for the ranch over to Phin. He's going to have to pull his weight until I can figure out what to do. Besides, family men get precedence in this situation."

"Your parents are going to be upset," Lily said.

"Land is just land," Sam said, "but fatherhood is everything. I've got to design a Santa suit."

Lily sighed. "The babies won't even know it's Christmas this year."

"Yes," Sam said, "but my father is a determined old soul, too. And every Christmas Eve, he climbed up to my window and tapped on it, with a big ho, ho, ho!" The memory of it made Sam happy. "I'm going to love being a dad. And a husband, though not a bossy one. I got the message."

"Good," Lily said.

Sam pulled up in front of the hospital, sliding the truck into the no-parking zone. He helped her down and an attendant came to assist her.

It wasn't until Sam watched Lily slowly walk into the hospital that he realized he hadn't told her that he loved her. Wasn't the husband supposed to bring his wife a special gift in the hospital, to thank her for giving him a child? In Lily's case, times four.

For an expectant father, he was doing very sloppy work, he decided. She was in good hands inside the hospital, and the babies wouldn't come immediately. There was nothing he could do now.

But he needed to start out his husbanding role properly. He just didn't know how to show Lily how much he wanted to spend his entire life with her, and their new family.

A horse and sleigh-style buggy went by, wreathed with garlands and red bows and jingling bells, sending cold water from the recent rain splashing up onto the curb. The family inside waved at him, and he waved his hat back at them. The husband and wife laughed, the four kids grinned, and even the driver smiled under his stiff mustache.

That was how he wanted his family to be in five years.

Happy together.

Sam steered his truck back out onto the main street to head into town.

Chapter Eight

"Where's Sam?" Lily asked the nurse who was checking her pulse.

"I believe out parking." The nurse smiled at her. "He'll be here soon."

Lily hoped so. The pains were fierce and she was more nervous than she'd thought she'd be. But she wasn't as nervous as when he'd returned to Union Junction, when she'd been afraid that he'd be angry with her for not telling him about the pregnancy.

A baby *had* been part of their original bargain. She'd wanted him so much—and it had hurt incredibly when he'd left after finding out about her relations.

Part of her thought that she should have told him in the beginning, but then she remembered how much he despised her family, and she knew there wouldn't have even been a first "date," much less these children she was about to give birth to.

"Sam?" she called. The nurse had left the room, and Lily felt certain Sam should have been here by now. Laying her head back against the pillow, she wondered what her father would do when he arrived.

Lily could almost hear him licking his chops about getting Falling Hills Ranch. Her greatest fear now was that Sam was never going to believe that she hadn't set him up from the beginning.

But when Sam had told her he was going to tell Phin he had to run the ranch, and that he was staying in Union Junction with her, Lily knew she'd probably put all the aces in her father's hand. Her father might finally achieve his goal of getting Falling Hills. All because of her.

That knowledge hurt worse than the birth pains she was suffering.

And soon she'd have to face her parents, because Delilah had called her folks on their cell to tell them Lily was in labor. They were already in Texas and headed to the hospital.

The nurse came back into the room, with a doctor following her. "Here is Mrs. Johnston," the nurse said.

Lily blinked. "Mrs. Johnston?"

"Yes." The doctor looked at her chart. "Are you Mrs. Johnston?"

"I…am," she said slowly. Her ears rang at being addressed that way for the first time. "Yes. I am Lily *Johnston*."

"And I'm Sam Johnston," Sam said, striding into the room. "Hello, Doctor. You look beautiful, Lily," he said, kissing her on the forehead.

"You always say that," Lily said, her heart beating more quickly now that Sam was near.

"And it's always true." Sam looked at the doctor. "Is Lily all right?"

"I think we're going to have babies by nightfall," the doctor replied. "I want to watch her a little longer and do an examination. But you're a bit ahead of schedule, Mrs. Johnston. I'm not sure these babies are going to stay in much longer."

"She was supposed to go on bed rest today," Sam said. "Moving today was too stressful. In the future, she won't even get out of her chair."

Lily looked at the doctor. "I walked from one room to another room at my new house. I neither carried anything nor picked up so much as a glass of water. He's being far too overprotective. Try not to listen."

The doctor smiled. "Papa Bear."

"Exactly."

Sam crossed his arms. "That's my job."

Lily laid her head back on the pillow. "And then again, sometimes I like the way you do your job."

Sam glanced at the doctor, his eyes worried. "She's in a lot of pain. Can you do something for her?"

Dr. Adams smiled. "I like you, Mr. Johnston. Most husbands are not this involved. Could you do me a favor?"

"Sure," Sam said eagerly.

"Would you mind stepping down to the cafeteria and getting me a cup of coffee? Maybe for about an hour?"

Sam laughed. "Are you asking me to get lost?"

The doctor winked. "This next part is boring. I promise. You need to save your strength for when she really needs you."

"All right," Sam agreed. "But no pain."

The doctor grinned. Lily felt better just hearing Sam try to take care of her in his awkward way.

"I'll be right back," Sam said. "The doctor thinks I'm underfoot."

"In a good way," Lily said, then reached out for him. "Wait, Sam, I have to tell you something."

"Now, or after I get my cup, ah, the doctor's cup of coffee?"

"After," Dr. Adams insisted. "Babies first, then chitchat. I promise he'll remember where he parked his vehicle, Mrs. Johnston."

"It's actually not about parking," Lily said.

"You can't believe how many excited husbands we have come in here and either lock their keys in a still-running car or forget what they drove." The doctor laughed, the nurse shooed Sam from the room, and Lily hoped she wasn't too late to put things right with Sam.

THE HOSPITAL CAFETERIA was pleasant, with candy canes taped to the walls and painted gingerbread-men boards ringing the room. Sam's coffee was served in a mug with a Christmas wreath on it. He cooled his boots at a table that was covered with a white tablecloth with gold stars.

He liked Union Junction. It would be no hardship for him to settle here. The town was homey, the people friendly. Lily had a lot of friends who seemed quite welcoming. He could envision being happy here, even in a converted red schoolhouse. More so than at Falling Hills.

Taking over the ranch had never been his dream.

Now Lily was his dream. After all the searching he'd ever done, from state to state, in his heart he'd wanted a woman like her. She was strong, sassy, independent. A little wily, and he liked that, too, because it kept him on his toes. She was sexy, a hot pistol when it counted, and he really liked that. Adventurous. He loved her sense of adventure. How many women would marry a man with an upfront agreement? She'd taken the money he'd sent her as part of their agreement and very sensibly chosen a home that could be enlarged to fit their family, with plenty of land that could be fashioned to fit their needs.

He'd never feel hemmed in with what she'd chosen.

She was a startling woman, and he was crazy about her. He pulled a jeweler's box from his pocket, looking at it for a moment with a smile. Then he opened it, giving the necklace inside a satisfied nod. Four round diamonds, one for each baby, in a heart—his heart.

"I hope she appreciates your romantic side," an elderly lady behind him said. She was holding a lunch tray and peering over his shoulder, and Sam grinned at her. "Thank you."

"What a nice boy," she told her husband as they walked on. "I remember when you used to bring me things like that."

Sam looked at the couple, still enjoying each other after all their years together, shared memories bonding them.

He couldn't wait to get started with Lily.

Baby one, baby two, baby three, baby four. Four Texas babies, all his and Lily's.

He wanted to shout his joy to the sky.

"You can come to the room now," the friendly nurse who'd been in Lily's room said to him.

Sam jumped to his feet.

WHEN SAM GOT THERE, there were two people standing beside Lily's bed. Tucking the jeweler's box back into his pocket, he recognized Lily's parents.

"Hello," he said.

"Howdy," the man said. The woman nodded.

"Sam, you must know my parents, Clara and Fats Bartholomew. Mom, Dad, this is my husband, Sam Johnston."

The introduction could have been a firecracker going off in a room that fell uncomfortably silent.

"We're so proud of our little girl," Clara said. "Welcome to our family, Sam."

Sam swallowed.

Fats grinned. "We're looking forward to our families getting to know one another better."

Sam looked at the odd expression on Lily's face. A reunion for the black sheep? Forgiveness for the daughter who provided grandchildren?

"Thank you," Sam said simply. "I'm very proud of my wife."

They fell awkwardly silent again. Sam stared at the machines that had been put in place to monitor Lily and the babies.

"Yoo-hoo!" A woman peeked around the corner. "We're here!"

Sam's parents walked into the room, hesitating a second when they saw the Bartholomews. But then they hugged Sam, and his mom went right over to touch Lily's hand. "I'm Ida," she said. "Aren't you lovely. Sam, what a beautiful wife you found."

Lily smiled wanly. "Thank you."

"Clara, Fats," Ida said. "How was your flight?"

"Fine," Clara replied.

"Excellent." In her no-nonsense fashion, Ida turned to her husband. "Ralph, say hello to your daughter-in-law, and then let's get out from underfoot. Lily looks like she'd like to have some peace and quiet to deliver these babies."

Ralph did as he was told, then Ida shooed him from the room. "Well, come on," she told Fats. "Clara, don't you recognize a woman who wants to let out a good yell?"

In shock from the tiny peppery woman castigating them, the Bartholomews dutifully kissed their daughter and followed her from the room.

"Yikes," Sam said. "That was scary. How are you doing?"

"I'm fine. But I've been thinking. Sam, we're going to have to take control here."

"First, I think we need better communication skills."

"I do, too," Lily said. "I have to be honest, after seeing our families…I don't think this is going to work. Birthing isn't going to be the cleansing experience I thought it was."

"You haven't done it yet," Sam said. "Can I get you some ice chips or something?" He peered into a container. "I think that's what the nurse has here, but I don't know if it's for you or for me."

"Sam, pay attention," Lily said. "I want a divorce."

Chapter Nine

Lily lowered her gaze as Sam stared at her, obviously shocked. She knew she could never explain it to him, after all they'd been through. But it had been clear from the moment the room filled—too much animosity existed between their families, and she'd been unrealistic to think that grandchildren would make a difference.

Or even the Christmas season.

Worse had been the look in Sam's eyes when he'd seen her father. The question had been clear on his face: Had she married him to get Falling Hills for her father? The black sheep making good? With them married—and Sam down here with her, and Phin not wanting to run the ranch—what reason did the Johnstons have not to accept Fats Bartholomew's offer?

Particularly if the Johnstons wanted to be close to their grandchildren.

She couldn't bear it another moment. Their marriage had been based on an agreement—and agreements could be broken.

It would hurt her to lose Sam. But family was family, and hers was no easy thing to deal with.

"Divorce?" Sam said. "No way. You Bartholomews are going to stick to one deal in your lives, and the one you're going to stick to is the one *you* made with *me*."

And then he left the room.

"It's time," the nurse said, walking into the room. "Do you want me to get your husband? I saw him going down the hall. We're going to wheel you down for your caesarian now. Do you want your mother?"

"No, thank you," Lily said. That was the last person she wanted. In spite of everything, in spite of how impossible their marriage was, she only wanted Sam by her side. She wanted him to tease her and make her laugh so she wouldn't be so scared.

She wanted to see his face when he saw his children for the first time.

Suddenly, she felt a big hand take hold of hers as she was being rolled down the hall. Sam looked down at her, big and strong and handsome, and instantly, Lily knew he understood.

"I'll be here when you come out," Sam said.

She thought she heard him say *I love you*.

"I love you, too," she murmured, closing her eyes. "But you'll be happier without me in your life."

SAM STOOD, ASTONISHED BY what Lily had said. She loved him. But she thought he'd be happier without her.

"She won't remember a thing she said," the nurse said. "You'd be surprised what women say to their husbands before they deliver. You know that expression 'What happens is Vegas stays in Vegas'?"

Did he ever. "We were married in Vegas."

"Then you'll appreciate that most of what's said during the birth process should probably be deleted from the memory bank."

"You think?"

The nurse nodded. "I know. If you'd heard half of the stuff I've heard over the years, you'd know why the fathers suffer just as much as the moms."

"Really?"

She patted his arm. "Go visit with your folks. Leave this part to us. I'll come get you when you have babies to hold."

He didn't want to leave Lily, but he supposed he should.

"They're in the cafeteria," she said.

"Thanks." Heading off, he found his parents sitting at a table with the Bartholomews—and everybody arguing like crazy. "Hey!" he said. "This is a birthday, not a battleground."

The four adults looked at him.

"Mr. Bartholomew thinks you and Lily should go live with them," Ida said. "I told him you would do no such thing."

Sam blinked. "We live in a converted schoolhouse. Here, in Union Junction."

His dad looked at him. "You're not moving back to Montana?"

"No." Sam shook his head. "I'm sorry, Dad. This has all happened fairly quickly, or I would have told you sooner. My family is here. So I'm staying."

Fats beamed. "My offer's still open. Anytime."

Ralph glared at him. "I still have one more son."

"One who's more interested in the recreational side of life," Fats pointed out.

"And I've had other offers," Ralph said.

"I'm willing to top the best offer you get by twenty per-cent," Fats said.

"Fats," Sam said, "did it ever occur to you that you can't buy everything you want?"

"No," Fats said. "And if I ever get that notion in my head, Clara's promised to take me out behind the woodshed and shoot me."

"No, I haven't," Clara said, sitting up. "That would not look good in the papers."

"Anyway," Sam said, "it's Christmas. Let's talk about happy things."

"It's Christmas," his father said. "You may recall that the offer was only good until Christmas."

"So tell them no," Sam said.

"We're related now, honey," Ida said. "We're trying to do this in the spirit of family."

Sam glared at his new father-in-law. "Mr. Bartholomew, I'd like your daughter's hand in marriage."

"You've got it, son." Fats beamed. "In fact, I'm glad you do."

"There." He looked at his parents. "That's all I ever owed him. And you owe him nothing."

"Sam, we're going to have four grandchildren. It's important for the in-laws and the out-laws to get along, for the sake of the babies," Ida said. "But if you're going to settle here, then that puts us in more of a mind to consider their offer seriously. It is a lot of money, Sam."

Fats grinned. "What did you say about money not buying everything, son-in-law?"

Sam nodded. "I'll remember that."

Uneasy silence settled around the table.

"Merry Christmas," Sam told the four of them. Then he left the cafeteria, heading back to Lily—and the family he had created with her.

FIVE HOURS LATER, SAM stared through a nursery window at the four babies sleeping in the neonatal unit. Never in his life had he ever thought that his heart could be so full. Knowing that he was going to become a father was no preparation for actually seeing his children.

It was the most wonderful Christmas present he could ever have. His heart filled with love for Lily, for giving him these gifts.

"What do you think about those little babies?" his mother asked, coming to stand beside him.

"I can hardly take it in," Sam said.

"Are they boys or girls?" his father asked.

"I don't know. The white blankets don't give much away. And the name cards say Baby Johnston, which I like. But I don't care if they're boys or girls," Sam said. "I'm just so glad they're here."

"You'd better go see Lily," Ida said. "I saw them wheeling her into her room."

He felt the jeweler's box in his pocket. "Yes, I should go see her." But he didn't move away from the window.

"Don't let us spoil your biggest day, son," Ida said. "The Bartholomews and us get along just fine, in our own way. We understand our relationship. Your father and I have tried to influence you enough. Don't feel like you have to make any decisions based on us." She patted his back. "All that really matters are in those blankets, and down the hall."

Sam nodded. "I want to do the right thing for you, too."

"Yes, but your family is here now." Ida smiled up at him. "We're proud of you, Sam. And we like Lily."

"I do, too."

His father nodded. "Your mother's right. Everything will work out the way it should with Falling Hills, but we sure are delighted to be grandparents. That matters most of all to us."

Sam blinked. "Lily wants to divorce me. She doesn't think we'll ever be able to rise above who we are. Who she is."

"Well, Mr. Bartholomew may be a tough old bird," Ralph said, "but so is your mother."

Ida laughed. "Don't let your father fool you. He's not going to be railroaded by Fats."

"Clara will talk bad about you all over town," Sam said.

"As if I care what anybody thinks." Ida shrugged. "We'll sell when and if we're good and ready. This offer will have to elapse, because we've decided to do something different."

"Have you?" Sam asked.

"Yes. We need to keep our ranch for your children," Ralph said. "Our grandchildren. They need their heritage."

Sam hesitated. "I thought it was too much work for you."

"It is, if no one's going to enjoy it but us," Ida said. "But we look forward to seeing your grandchildren enjoy the place we've all loved so long."

"What?" Fats said, coming up behind them.

"We're not selling, Fats," Ralph said. "Thank you for your generous offer."

"You can't do that!" Fats stated loudly. "We had a deal!"

"We were only considering a deal. Ida and I are going to keep our place for our grandchildren."

So much for Fats waiting it out, Sam thought, calculating how long Fats would have to wait for the grandchildren to grow up so he could make another offer. He had to smile.

"I'll up my offer—"

"Fats," Ida said, "we're not interested. No matter the price."

"This is all your fault," Fats said angrily to Sam. "You got my daughter, and now the property I wanted."

"Deal with it," Sam said. "You've got four grandchildren."

"Yeah, but—" Fats turned to face the window briefly, then did a double take. "Four Johnstons?"

Sam frowned. "Didn't Lily tell you?"

"We were only told she was pregnant," Clara said. "Oh, my goodness, Fats. Aren't they darling?"

Fats stared in shock through the window. "Four," he muttered.

Clara tugged at his arm. "Are you all right, Fats?"

A nurse checked on each baby, then put little red knit stocking caps on each one. They looked like tiny Santas hibernating in plastic pods.

"I can't believe it," Fats said. "That's the most amazing thing I ever saw."

Sam watched Fats's shoulders lose their defensive posture. His wife looped her arm through his. It was like watch-

ing the Christmas spirit soften one of the hardest hearts—
Scrooge being charmed by baby love.

It made Sam smile, and softened his heart, too.

Fats wiped a tear from his eye, though he hid it carefully.
"Excuse me," he said. "I need to talk to my daughter."

He disappeared, with Clara hurrying along beside him.

Ida hugged her son, and Ralph put his arm around the two
of them. They stood there for a long time, looking through the
window at the little red-capped Christmas miracles that would
change their lives.

If Lily wanted to leave him, he decided, it would break
his heart.

But if she wanted out of their original agreement, he would
let her go. For the sake of those little bundles in front of him,
he would do everything to help their mother be happy.

A divorce was not what he wanted for Christmas—but if
it was what Lily wanted, he would make that agreement, too.

Chapter Ten

"Lily," Fats said, "how are you feeling?"

Lily turned her head to look at her parents. "Where are the babies?"

"In the neonatal unit," Clara said. "They're so sweet, Lily."

"Where's Sam?" Lily shifted, feeling strange now that all the babies were out of her tummy. She missed Sam. She wanted to talk to him as soon as possible.

"Lily, I have something to tell you," her father said.

"What is it, Dad?"

He cleared his throat. "We're very glad Sam invited us down here to share Christmas with you and your new family."

Lily looked at her father. "Do you mean that?"

"Absolutely." Fats nodded vehemently. "Lily, I—"

Lily waited.

"Lily, I'm sorry," Fats said, taking hold of her hand. "I have treated your husband and his family badly. I hope you can forgive me."

Lily was stunned. "Dad, I don't know what to say."

"They're fine people, they really are. I'm a greedy old man who tries to fill his life up with things. But I plan to do better, if you'll give me another chance."

She swallowed, taking a second to think about what her father had said. "Thank you for your sweet words. They mean a lot to me. But there's someone else who's part of my life now, and I don't know if he will be as forgiving. You'll really have to talk to Sam."

"Did I hear my name?" Sam demanded, walking into the room.

Fats drew himself up tall. "Son-in-law," he said, "I've been an ass."

Sam glanced at Lily. "No arguments here."

Fats nodded. "I hope you and your family can forgive my actions. I'd like to be as much a part of those babies' lives as you can stand. I promise to be a changed man."

Sam looked at Lily again, to see if he was missing something. Lily smiled and shrugged at her husband, her heart singing that her father was so clearly sincere. The babies *had* made a difference for her family. If Fats and the Johnstons could work things out after all these years, maybe she and Sam could work things out, too.

"How can I begin to show you that I mean my words?" Fats said.

"Well," Sam said, "first you can leave me alone with my bride."

Fats marched to the door with Clara right behind him.

"And Fats," Sam said, his eyes on Lily, "there'll be a Christmas dinner at the schoolhouse, prepared by me. Lily and I would appreciate it if you and Clara could plan on being there. Hopefully, the babies will be home by then."

Fats nodded. "We'll bring the pecan pie. Thank you, son-in-law."

"Name's Sam," Sam said. "We can be friends now."

"Sam." Fats waved, then left Sam and Lily alone.

"Well done," Sam said to Lily, coming to give her a kiss on the forehead. "There are four adorable little peppermints out in the neonatal nursery."

"Peppermints?"

"Red caps, white blankets. Very small. But quite healthy, apparently." Sam grinned at her. "How do you feel, little mother?"

"How do you feel, big daddy?"

"Exhausted." Sam sat down on the bed next to her, picking up her hand. "Resolving all that emotional debris is tiring."

Lily smiled. "You handled it so well."

Sam shrugged. "I have to live up to my wife, who can deliver four babies and still wear a smile. So, about that thing you said to me before they wheeled you into delivery—"

"Didn't you listen to the nurse?" Lily said. "What gets said in delivery, stays in delivery."

Sam laughed. "She told you, did she?"

Lily nodded. "I was having a panic moment."

"Don't have any more of those. I couldn't bear it if you left me."

"Even after everything, you're still going to stay with me and the babies? You're not taking over the ranch?"

"Lily, I would never leave you. I love you. In fact, I have a token of my appreciation. Though I still think you should marry me again, I will go along with your theory of the birth process as being the most special bonding experience we can share. So from mere arranged marriage to the real thing, I wanted you to have a small, sparkly something to commemorate our elaborate, four-baby ceremony."

Pulling out the jeweler's box, Sam gave it to her. Lily reached for it, and he pulled it back, grinning. He handed it to her again; she reached for it, and he pulled it back.

"Sam!" Lily said, laughing.

"I just wanted to be certain you really want me this time," Sam said. "This time, there's no agreement. No ranch to keep, no independence to win, just me and you and those babies, being a real family."

She gave him a sly look, then snatched the box from his

hand, opening it quickly. "Oh, Sam," she said. "It's the most beautiful thing I've ever received."

"Nah, those are down the hall. The little peppermints. I still don't know their gender, though." He got up next to her on the bed and gave her a long kiss. "I love you, Lily. Thank you for my children, whatever they are."

"I love you too, Sam. I'm sorry for what I said, and what I didn't say. Two boys, two girls, and what difference does gender make, I say, when they're all going to be wearing Wrangler jeans, anyway?"

"Do they have names?"

"I was thinking Mason, because he helped us start the salon and he's been such a good friend, and Phin because you love him. I was thinking Tisha and Violet, because they're my best friends out of all my fellow stylists. Those are not ordinary names, which will suit our family fine. All parental names such as Clara, Ida, Ralph and Fats I would suggest for middle names…"

"Nah," Sam said. "Let's just start over fresh."

"So Phineas Samuel works for you?" Lily asked with a twinkle in her eyes.

"Yes." He grinned. "You've changed my life. You've changed my family's, and yours, all for the better. Merry Christmas, *Mrs.* Johnston. I loved you from the moment you first sassed me, and I'll always be in love with you, too much for words."

"Merry Christmas, *Mr.* Johnston," Lily said, her heart singing as she held her forever-husband tight.

ON CHRISTMAS EVE, Sam put on jeans, a red western shirt, and a Santa hat to cook a turkey in the smoker out back of the schoolhouse, which Samson kept an eager eye on. Lily put on a matching Santa hat, and a holly-flecked dress, and then Sam slowly escorted her to the candlelit table. Both the Johnstons and the Bartholomews ate a peaceful dinner, enjoying getting to know one another.

It was a Christmas of firsts, which is what Christmas is meant to be.

And in bassinets beside the tree, in their red caps and white blankets, four little peppermints slept quietly, completely unaware that they were the reason for the merriest Christmas their families had ever known.

A TEXAN
UNDER THE MISTLETOE
Leah Vale

Dear Reader,

Tradition. In my dictionary, tradition is roughly defined as the handing down of customs and beliefs from generation to generation by word of mouth or practice. In my family, tradition means fattigmann. For those of you without any Viking longboats docked at your family tree, fattigmann is a traditional Norwegian Christmas cookie. A pain to make, not to mention a little dangerous with all that boiling oil, but it wouldn't be Christmas without fattigmann.
Or would it?

I decided to explore the notion of traditions in this story, creating one character, Lori Beth Whittaker, for whom traditions equal security, and another, Jackson Hooper, who finds nothing but painful reminders in the traditions synonymous with Christmas in Hoopers' Creek, Texas. Amidst the trying aftermath of a flood, can Lori show Jackson that there is nothing like down-home tradition to heal the heart?

Regardless of what traditions are important to you, be they generations old or brand spanking new, may they bring you peace, joy and love this holiday season.

Happy holidays!

Leah Vale

For my mother for being a Christmas baking machine,
and for my aunt, Kathy Rohrer, for keeping
the fattigmann tradition alive for us.

Chapter One

"I'm sorry, Mrs. Perez, but there won't be a Hooper Creek Christmas festival this year."

Lori Whittaker stumbled against the people clad in rain slickers standing at the back of the Hooper Creek town meeting. Her attention was drawn to the man at the podium, whose answer to the question that was clearly on everyone's mind this December evening amounted to blasphemy in this little chunk of north-central Texas.

Considering who that man was, she couldn't possibly be the only one in the grange hall wondering if she'd heard right.

Lou Cambell stood off to her left, his green-and-black-plaid quilted jacket spattered with the same dun-colored muddy residue that coated the buildings on Main Street to knee height. He scratched his balding head. "No *Christmas festival* this year?" he asked, sounding confused.

A pair of strong hands that still had the power to set her blood racing gripped the podium. "That's right, Lou." Jackson Hooper, great-grandson of Hollis Hooper, the founding father of Hooper Creek and creator of the annual Hooper Creek Christmas festival, met the room's collective gasp with only a twitch of his unyielding jaw.

Those who didn't know him as well as Lori might miss the tension in the broad shoulders that had filled out since she'd last seen him ten years ago. Probably from carrying the burden of his late father's legacy this past year.

Sympathy squeezed Lori so hard she grimaced. What a blow Walter Hooper's fatal heart attack must have been for Jackson. If only she hadn't been in New Mexico when they'd held Walt's funeral. Dallas was far away enough as it was, but at least she could have reached Hooper Creek in time to pay her respects.

She may have even exchanged a word or two with Jackson. Offered him her understanding, her support, if he'd needed her.

Heck, there was a first time for everything.

Except, that is, for canceling Hooper Creek's Christmas festival. There'd never be a good reason for that. Especially not now, when there was so much emotional rebuilding to be done in the town.

What was Jackson thinking?

Using the playful phrase that had started many spirited discussions in their past, she called out, "That has to be the most harebrained thing you've ever suggested, Jackson Hooper."

Lou turned in her direction, his bushy gray eyebrows drawn together. "Who...?"

Lori could tell Jackson knew who had spoken. And his reaction wasn't the one she'd been hoping for. There was no exclamation of delight. Not even brows raised in pleasant surprise over her return. Though, she couldn't rightly claim his reaction was unexpected, considering the way they'd parted. He simply stiffened and his eyes, the exact deep green as her grandfather's endless fields of alfalfa she'd once sought to escape, narrowed, searching for her among those standing in the back.

No, she shouldn't be surprised he wasn't glad to see her. Not after she'd chosen the kind of life she had over him. She'd wanted to experience the world, but his world was Hooper Creek. And neither one of them was known for compromising.

"Lori Beth?" Her grandfather, Clifford Whittaker, turned and rose from his seat three rows from the front.

As the men who stood in front of her—one of grandpa's neighbors, Darrell Swanson, a short-haul trucker, and Jeff Hadridson, another rancher whose kids she used to occasionally baby-sit—shifted to look back at her, she stood up on her toes to compensate for being only five and a half feet tall. "Yes, it's me, Grandpa." She raised her hand. "Back here."

Grandpa adjusted his wire-rimmed glasses as if he didn't trust what he saw. "What are you doing here?"

Lori tugged her black sweater back down from where it had ridden up, and answered, "I—excuse me, Mr. Swanson, Mr. Hadridson." She squeezed her way forward. "I've come to help you, like I said I would."

"And I said there's no need," Grandpa blustered.

Painfully aware of the acute interest of what appeared to be the entire adult population of her hometown, most of whom she hadn't seen for ten years, she felt her throat threatening to close. "I've been by your place, Grandpa." She didn't have to say more. Nor could she keep the self-recrimination from her tone.

She shouldn't have believed him when he'd told her the small ranch she'd been raised on had been completely spared from the worst flood to hit Hooper Creek in a hundred years. He'd always been so willing to help her, but turned stubborn as a mule when she tried to give back. She should have known he wouldn't want to "bother" her, and take her away from her big-city life.

If only he knew how empty that life was.

After hearing from her grandfather and learning of his losses—she now knew they had been drastically underplayed—she'd looked around her downtown Dallas high-rise apartment and acknowledged there was nothing there she'd mourn if she'd been the one caught in a flood. Her modern,

Scandinavian-design furniture suddenly seemed spare and cold, not mature and independent. And she traveled too much for work to allow for pets, truly close friends or—she was startled to realize—clutter.

Even after being gone ten years, her strongest ties were to what she'd left behind in Hooper Creek.

She'd known then it was time to see if it was possible to truly go home again.

Determined to regain her place here, she raised her chin. "I've come to help. Any way I can."

Jackson interjected, "Then start by keeping your opinions to yourself."

Lori countered, "Considering the cancellation of the Christmas festival harebrained isn't an opinion, it's a fact. How can you not see that the festival is exactly what this town needs right now after being ravaged by the worst storm—"

"Storms," Jackson corrected.

"All right, *storms* to hit here in a century? I think the traditions from better days will give everyone a much-needed sense of normalcy." And a sense of security from ties that couldn't be swept away in a muddy torrent. The same security Lori discovered she didn't have in her big-city life.

The ties she desperately wanted back.

Nodding until her short graying black curls bobbed, Mrs. Perez said, "Amen," and tugged closed the front of her vibrant red southwestern-style jacket.

The line of Jackson's mouth grew as foreboding as the sky before a gully washer. "Repairing the water main will do that better than any festival."

Outbursts of agreement, mostly masculine, punctuated Jackson's statement.

But various words of disagreement sounded loudly enough to encourage Lori. She moved up the center aisle a few steps. "I'd wager the annual Christmas festival was held long before this town even had a water main." She spread her arms wide and appealed to the rows of people she'd known most of her life. "And who says we can't do both?"

"I do," Jackson answered.

Baffled, she let her arms go limp at her sides. "How can you, when your own father—"

"That's enough, Lori." Jackson moved from behind the podium and stormed down the aisle toward her, the heels on his worn black cowboy boots pounding against the grange's rough wooden floor.

She stood stuck like a fence post when she probably should have backed away, because the memory of Jackson Hooper in all his denim-clad glory was nothing compared to the reality.

Two years her senior, he'd been young, gorgeous and confident when she'd left town seeking confidence of her own. The intervening ten years and everything they'd held had turned him into a stunning man, hardened less by certainty than a gritty determination.

His blond hair had darkened. Weariness had deepened the grooves on his forehead and on either side of his full mouth, but his straight nose and square jaw looked the same as they did in her dreams.

When he reached her, he said in a low, rough voice, "Let's take this outside," and snagged her elbow. Without breaking stride, he pulled her around and hauled her back the way she'd come, only this time the crowd quickly parted to let them through.

He slowed just enough to say to Mr. Swanson, "See if you can get a list of names of those willing to pitch in and work on the main, will ya, Darrell? The county has turned off all the valves, so it's good to go."

Mr. Swanson nodded. "Sure, Jackson." There wasn't so much as a flicker of concern for her in his dark brown eyes despite the fact Jackson was bodily removing her from the premises.

Lori glanced over her shoulder at her grandpa, but he was speaking with an animated Mrs. Perez. No one appeared particularly worried that little bitty her was being escorted outside by great big Jackson Hooper.

Probably because she'd spent the end of her senior year in high school and every summer and holiday home from Southern Methodist University in Dallas hanging on his strong arm. And now he was the area's most influential rancher, inheriting the role from his father.

Or maybe they just thought she deserved whatever she was going to get for butting in after being gone for so long.

Lori doubted many knew that once she'd moved away, her grandpa had insisted on being the one to visit her, claiming he needed a change of scenery from the isolated town of Hooper Creek now and again. Sadly, thanks to her constant traveling for work—visiting various airports to check on the quality of Southern Skyway's ticketing agents' performance—Grandpa hadn't visited often enough.

Deep down, she suspected he didn't want her making the long drive between Dallas and Hooper Creek, so rife with horrible memories for her. As if his making the drive was any better. Although, at least, more often than not, he caught a ride with Darrell Swanson when the trucker hauled stock to the city in his big rig.

Jackson led her through the door and onto the covered wooden boardwalk outside the small grange hall. As on most of Main Street, the boardwalk's planks were so warped from water damage they resembled an undulating fun-house bridge. Thanks to the gathering fog, the dank smell of creek backwater was heavy in the air.

She still had a hard time comprehending the extent of the damage to the area. The wide, meandering creek the town shared its name with was normally shallow and docile. But this was Texas; even the creeks knew how to do it up big every now and again. Which meant taking out every sweet gum, live oak and hickory within reach—even the pecan trees that used to line her grandpa's drive—leaving them broken and upended with their roots washed naked and their branches wedged beneath the boardwalk or jammed against the buildings.

Though the door swung closed behind them, Jackson didn't stop until they were several uneven steps away from the entrance. He released her and planted his hands on his hips. "What was all that about, Lori?"

"Hello, to you, too, Jackson. I've been fine, thanks for asking." She made a show of rubbing her elbow, despite the fact he hadn't hurt her.

His nostrils flared. "I repeat, what was that all about?"

Lori sighed. The road home was not paved with sarcasm. She had to remember to curb her tongue in the future—yet she didn't regret her words in the grange. This year especially she craved the traditions of Christmas more than anything. Well, almost anything. Her gaze automatically went to Jackson's mouth. The disapproval she found there snapped her back to the moment.

She crossed her arms over her chest. "Exactly what I said. Cancelling the festival is a harebrained idea."

"In case you haven't noticed—" he waved a hand at the mud- and water-stained buildings and piles of flood debris next to the battered boardwalk "—this isn't exactly a laughing matter."

She turned her head in the direction he indicated and saw a green canoe that had been left "parked" in front of the barber shop, tied to the hitching post that had been preserved through the years along with the building's Old West facade. She closed her eyes for a second and took a deep breath of moist, rank air. "I know. Which is exactly why you can't cancel Hooper Creek's Christmas festival. The people of this town *need* it, Jackson."

His hands dropped to his sides. "What the people need is to concentrate their efforts on cleaning up and rebuilding." He turned away from her to look out at the battered, lone main drag of little Hooper Creek. Not all that much had changed since his great-grandfather's era, the town's heyday. "They don't have the time or energy to waste on some festival."

"It's not just *some festival,* Jackson. It's the Christmas festival. The one that brings everyone into town together for a few nights a year, regardless of beliefs or cultural background, and makes everyone feel as if they belong to something bigger and better."

That was what it had done for her. She'd been all of nine years old when that tire had flown off a truck and smashed into her family's car. Her mom and dad had been killed instantly. Alone in the back, Lori had been unhurt. Physically, at least. She'd been so lost and alone after the accident. The people of Hooper Creek had stepped in, but only as an adult did she recognize the value of what this town had given her.

She hesitated a moment, wondering if she should risk saying more. She wanted to reach out and touch Jackson, but the fact that she'd left stood between them, so she settled for speaking gently. "The Christmas festival is part of your father's legacy."

Jackson whirled toward her, his green eyes blazing. "I am very aware of what my father's legacy is, Lori. I certainly don't need you to remind me. Just as I don't need you butting in when I'm trying to organize work parties."

Never one to be cowed, she planted her fists on her hips, mimicking his earlier stance. "Organizing work parties has nothing to do with the Christmas festival."

He leaned toward her. "It does when the same able bodies are needed to make both happen."

Her skin warmed at his nearness. She raised her chin and pretended she wasn't aware of the flush spreading on her cheeks. "Who says they can't do both?"

"Who says asking too much of people won't break their backs once and for all, and drive them away for good?"

Her anger left her in a rush. "Is that what you're afraid of? That people will move away from Hooper Creek?"

He straightened, his chest expanding as he took a deep breath. "Like I said, I'm well aware of the legacy my father, and his father, and his father before, left for me. I can only ask so much of the people around here."

Clearly he cared about this town and its inhabitants, but there was more to his argument than concern—he considered himself responsible for them. His shoulders weren't *that* broad.

She squared her own shoulders. "Then I'll do it."

"Do what?"

"Put on the festival. I'll make it happen."

"I thought you came back to help your grandpa."

"I did. I'm going to. But I can do both."

He stared at her for a long moment, then faced the street again. Jackson remained silent for so long she was about to repeat herself, but before she could he said, "No."

Truly confounded by his stubbornness, she asked, "Why?"

"It'll be a distraction we don't need right now."

"Says you."

"That's right." He turned, leveling a finger at himself and glaring down at her. "I'm not the one who took off for a more exciting life, who hasn't lived through the last few brutal storms and their aftermath."

The recrimination was not entirely deserved—she'd been seeking herself, not excitement—but she swallowed her pride and offered simply, "I'm here now."

"Yeah, but for how long?"

She wanted to shout *forever,* only now she really wasn't so sure anymore. Not if she'd never be welcomed by the one person whose acceptance she needed the most. The vacation time she'd piled up from her job would allow her to stay through the holidays. Maybe by then she'd know.

Her hesitation was damning. Jackson scoffed. "I thought as much. Don't fill your plate with more than you plan on finishing during your little Christmas vacation, Lori Beth." He turned and went back into the grange hall, the door slamming behind him.

Tears welled unexpectedly in her eyes. She'd always been just Lori to Jackson, not Lori Beth, the sad little girl raised by her widowed grandpa after her parents were killed in a car crash on their way to Hooper Creek from Dallas. As she'd struggled to become a woman in her own right, her full name occasionally struck her as condescending.

Maybe Jackson was right. Maybe she couldn't go home again.

JACKSON HOOPER BARELY heard the arguments going on around him as he made his way back to the podium at the front of the grange hall his great-grandfather had built. Certainly, whatever he'd said to Darrell Swanson had been gibberish when Darrell had handed him the list of names for the water main work party. His brain was too full with Lori Whittaker. She was back in town—and obviously not for long.

By all rights, time should have dulled the ache she'd left him with, but it seemed pain was the only thing he was capable of feeling anymore.

If only time hadn't been kind to Lori, turning her from a pretty, spunky girl with the world at her fingertips to a gorgeous, fiery woman who, according to her grandpa, was used to having the world beneath her thumb.

She wore her thick brown hair longer and stick-straight, the lighter strands framing her face undoubtedly artfully placed by a high-priced stylist rather than by the sun, as when she was younger. Her petite figure had matured—her breasts, which he remembered a little too well, were fuller beneath her black turtleneck sweater, and her hips curved her jeans nicely—and she'd lost the roundness in her cheeks.

The shadows he'd been so determined to banish all those years ago still darkened her blue eyes, but with some shadows of his own now, he recognized how arrogant he'd been. He could never have the power to wipe away her grief any more than someone could erase his.

He shouldn't be more attracted to her than he'd been back when he'd thought they wanted the same things out of life, when he'd thought daydreams were actual plans for the future. He shouldn't have to struggle to brush off her concern for him and the town she'd left behind.

And he definitely shouldn't have been seized with the urge to snatch her up into his arms and bury his face in her hair until this first Christmas without his father was long past.

He should *not* still have a weakness for Lori Whittaker.

This time, though, he wouldn't allow himself to get kicked in the teeth by the only woman with the power to truly hurt him.

Chapter Two

Weary from a morning spent scrubbing her grandfather's cupboards where he hadn't been able to reach, Lori stepped up onto the Hoopers' front porch. Memories crashed over her with near-staggering force.

Wisely built on high ground three generations ago, the house and the outbuildings had been spared from the flood. The ranch itself was large enough that their cattle had plenty of places to escape the rising water.

The white-washed covered porch with its two-person swing looked exactly as it had the last time she'd seen it, down to the evergreen swags hung from the posts and the painted wooden Santa propped next to the front door.

Exactly as it had when she'd told a young man she wanted to discover if life held more than what could be found in Hooper Creek by taking a job she'd been offered in Dallas. The same young man who'd refused time and again when she'd asked him to explore the world outside the town with her. His father had been alive then and Jackson could have easily taken off for a while. But he didn't want to leave, saw no need.

The older Lori grew, all she could think was: *Was staying in Hooper Creek what her parents had wanted for her?* They'd moved to Dallas, hadn't they?

When she'd broached the subject of going away with Jackson, he'd barely said a word. He'd merely wished her luck, then got up off the swing and gone inside the big old ranch house. His reaction had confirmed what she'd suspected—he hadn't cared for her as much as she'd hoped. His tie to the land had been stronger than his tie to her.

So she'd let it go, accepting a job she'd been recruited for while at SMU that involved travel, despite the hurt that still ached within her. Had she made a mistake?

She shook her head as she raised a hand to knock on the screen door's wooden frame. The time away had made her stronger and shown her the value of what was to be had here in this little town. The thing that had made her parents return again and again. The value of tradition. If she'd never left, she wouldn't be so sure about what she wanted now.

With her goal in mind, she quickly checked the red sweater and jeans she'd changed into for any mud.

The front door opened and Jackson's mother, Patsy Hooper, appeared. She still wore her hair short, but now it was more salt than pepper. She had on a holly-berry print apron over a green turtleneck and blue jeans.

"Lori Beth! As I live and breathe!" Patsy pushed open the screen door and stood on the threshold. "I must have had five phone calls this morning telling me you were back, but I have to say I was having a hard time believing it."

Fearing Patsy's opinions regarding Lori's return would echo her son's, Lori tentatively asked, "Why is that, Mrs. Hooper?"

Her barely lined face softened with motherly pride. "Because you always were destined for greater things, sweetheart."

Warmed by the unexpected praise, Lori looked at her boot-clad feet. "I wouldn't exactly call a low-level managerial position with an airline a *greater thing*."

"But your job has let you see the world, hasn't it?"

Lori had once thought it would. "Just the southwestern region of the United States."

Patsy grinned. "Well, that's a heck of a lot more than what I've seen. One of these days I'll have to remedy that. Come on in, hon." She stepped back and gestured to the welcoming foyer with its white wainscoting and colorful hand-knotted rug. "I was just working on the Christmas cookies I started yesterday but didn't finish because I got hit with one of my headaches. That's why I missed the town meeting last night. I was laid out on the couch with a washrag over my eyes."

"You're still having those? I'm so sorry, Mrs. Hooper."

She waved off Lori's concern, but the glow on her face let Lori know it was appreciated. "They only stop me for a little while. And please, call me Patsy. It makes me feel too old to have another grown woman call me Mrs. Hooper." Her hazel eyes suddenly glistening, she reached out and squeezed Lori's upper arm. "It's so good to see you, Lori Beth. You've blossomed into a stunning woman. Clifford certainly hasn't been exaggerating when he brags about you."

Regret stabbed Lori at the mention of her grandpa's devotion to her, and she could only shyly smile her thanks. She should have been around for him more these past years. How could she have taken so much for granted?

Determined to never make such a mistake again, Lori said in a rush, "I'm so sorry about Walt, Patsy. I was in Albuquerque when Grandpa called to tell me about his passing, and I couldn't get away—"

Patsy raised a hand. "Hush, honey. It's all right. I understand. To be honest, I probably wouldn't have noticed if you'd been here, anyway." She shook her head. "It was not a good time." As she touched Lori's face, her smile turned bittersweet. "The fact that you were thinking of us is enough."

Lori's eyes burned. "You were always like a mother to me, Patsy. You know that, don't you?"

The older woman sniffed softly and nodded, then grinned. "But Jackson would be your brother then, and we can't have that, now, can we?" Patsy effectively broke the somber mood. She motioned toward the hall. "Come on back and keep me company while I work on my cookies."

Patsy led the way down the white-paneled hall decorated with familiar photos to the bright, farm-style kitchen. The heavenly scent of fresh-baked cookies filled Lori's head with wonderful memories and her soul with contentment. Here was a prime example of the power of traditions.

Over her shoulder, Patsy asked, "Are you in town for the holidays?"

"Yes. And to help. I had quite a bit of vacation and sick leave built up that I needed to use before the end of the year. I came as soon as I found out how badly the town had been hit by this last flood."

Patsy went to the butcher-block island in the center of the kitchen, where an open jar of jam waited next to at least two dozen thumbprint cookies, cooling on racks. "Can't say that I'm surprised Clifford kept the amount of damage from you. He's never wanted to burden you."

Lori stopped on the opposite side of the island. "But I'm his only family. Helping him now that I'm a capable adult is the least I can do to repay him for giving me such a wonderful childhood." The contentment fled, and she realized how deeply it hurt her that her grandpa hadn't so much as sought her comfort after the flood.

She would prove to him that she'd always be there for him from now on. Just as he'd always been there for her.

"Your grandfather just wants you happy, Lori Beth."

Lori leaned a hip against the butcher block. "I know. And being here makes me happy."

Patsy smiled, her eyes warm. "Good to hear."

Lori watched Patsy drop teaspoons of strawberry jam into the cookies for a moment, then glanced around the kitchen for signs of the huge lunch Patsy always made for her son and husband to get them through the rest of the day working the ranch.

Granted, with Walt gone, Patsy only had Jackson to cook for, and the flood had disrupted normal operations, but Lori was sure Patsy would still insist on tending to her son's needs.

All Lori saw were racks filled with traditional Christmas baking.

She had no choice but to come right out and ask about her reason for coming here. "Um, are you expecting Jackson for lunch, Mrs. Ho…Patsy?"

The older woman gave Lori a startled look. "Oh! You came to see Jackson?"

Before Lori could assure her she wanted to see her, also, Patsy smiled and nodded. "That's right." She pointed the goopy spoon at Lori. "Juanita mentioned you two went at it during the town meeting." Patsy's smile turned soft and knowing and made Lori's skin prickle.

Returning her attention and the messy spoon to the cookies, Patsy said, "Nowadays, unless Jackson has been working right around here, he goes home and fixes his own lunch. Claims he's too old for me to be waiting on him." She snorted. "Frankly, I think it's because he believes *I'm* too old."

Lori blinked. "He goes *home?*" She couldn't imagine Jackson ever living anywhere other than the Circle H ranch. He loved it here. She'd initially gone off to SMU to learn how to help him successfully run the ranch, if he were to ever ask her. Had he changed so much?

Patsy raised her eyebrows at Lori. "Clifford didn't tell you?" She waved away the question. "I suppose he had no reason to."

Her casual dismissal of Lori and Jackson's past relationship, a relationship Lori herself had ended, inexplicably hurt. Although nowhere near as much as Jackson's reaction to her homecoming and her desire to make sure the Christmas festival happened.

"I would have thought you'd known, since Jackson started planning his house long before you left for that job in Dallas." Patsy shrugged. "Anyway, Jackson built himself a house years ago up on the knoll overlooking the north pond. Which is actually more of a lake lately," Patsy mused as she scooped up more jam.

The knoll overlooking the north pond? No. He couldn't have…Lori's gaze automatically darted to the kitchen window, but the knoll couldn't be seen from here because of the barn. Which was precisely why she and Jackson used to make out up there.

Not noticing Lori's distress, Patsy continued. "And since the flood, he's been working around town instead of here at the ranch. I doubt he's even been stopping long enough to eat lunch, the poor baby."

Lori shook herself and tried to remain focused on finding Jackson and changing his mind about the festival instead of dwelling on the past. There was no point wasting this opportunity to talk to Jackson's mother.

Lori took a calming breath. "Did Juanita tell you what Jackson and I *went at it* about at the town meeting?"

The spoon paused. "Yes. The Christmas festival," she said softly. Her late husband's gift back to the community he'd loved.

Lori knew she needed to tread carefully. "Before the meeting, had Jackson discussed with you his intention to cancel the festival?"

Patsy took extra care filling the last cookie. "He mentioned he wanted to bring up the subject at the meeting. He's afraid it'll be too much on top of everything else that needs to be done."

As gently as she could, Lori asked, "What do you think?"

"I think Jackson has the town's best interest at heart."

Lori's stomach sank. "So you agree with him? You don't believe the people around here would be able to put on the festival?"

Patsy pursed her lips. "I think we've had enough taken away from us already."

Exaltation jolted through Lori. "Exactly! But Jackson says the town can't handle any more."

Patsy snorted. "There's nothing the people of this town can't accomplish when they put their minds to it."

Lori gripped the edge of the butcher-block island. "Are you saying you think we should go ahead with the Christmas celebration as usual?"

Jackson's mother set the spoon down and met Lori's gaze. "Yes, I am." She planted a fist on her hip in punctuation.

It was all Lori could do not to jump up and down in excitement. Having Patsy Hooper in her camp was a major coup.

The stubborn set of Patsy's jaw, so reminiscent of her only child's, softened, and her fist slipped off her hip. "Though maybe pared down a bit. Trying to stage a wagon parade on that torn-up and mucky Main Street doesn't sound very smart, but there is no reason we can't hold the potluck and dance as usual."

"In your barn?" Lori asked, unable to keep the hope and excitement from her voice.

Patsy nodded. "In our barn."

Her choice of pronouns let Lori know that while Jackson might have built his own house, he still used the other outbuildings and had a say in the running of the ranch. She couldn't let his anger at her keep the festival from happening.

Just as she couldn't let the resulting hurt she felt keep her homecoming from being the new beginning she desperately wanted.

Lori did her best not to push Patsy too hard, because the woman was clearly torn between her loyalty to Jackson and to her husband's memory, but Lori needed clarification. "With the usual decorations?"

Grief clouded her eyes. "Walter wouldn't want it any other way."

Although tempered with sympathy, relief swept away the tension in Lori's body. "If you could spare a minute to show me where the decorations are stored, I can start hauling everything out and get it ready for people to come and help with putting them up. There isn't much time if we're going to have at least the potluck and dance part of the festival on the Saturday before Christmas as usual."

Nor did she have much time before Jackson discovered what she was up to. Once the barn was decorated, he'd *have* to let that part of the festival take place.

Wouldn't he?

"When I said no, I meant it, Lori," Jackson practically growled as he settled his cowboy hat more firmly on his head.

He immediately locked his teeth against the emotions that had blindsided him the second he'd stepped into the barn and saw Lori and his own mother hip-deep in opened boxes erupting with his father's beloved Christmas decorations.

Jackson had feared just the sight of the swags and ribbons and ornaments would hurt more than being trampled by his entire herd of cattle.

He'd been right.

He tried to shift his attention from the reminder of what he'd lost, to anger. Lori had completely ignored his wishes and gone behind his back to further her agenda. Enlisting his own mother's help was the lowest blow.

His mother sent him an unperturbed smile. "Well, hello, sweetheart. I figured you were in town again today. Did you decide to take a break and let me fix you lunch, after all?"

"No. I came to see if I could scrounge up a few more shovels. We've done as much as we can with the backhoes, but we don't want to risk damaging the water main further, so we're down to digging the old-fashioned way."

He looked pointedly at a red-cheeked Lori, ignoring how

appealing the heightened color made her. "Not easy work for people who've already spent the past weeks mopping out their own homes." He'd get it through her head one way or another that the town didn't have time for festivals of any sort.

Then he'd avoid her. Seeing her here, in his family's barn again, was almost too much to bear. He'd spent ten years burying the past deeper than any water main and had thought he'd never have to face it again. But here she was, making a liar out of him.

Lori looked away, her gaze dropping to the length of red velvet ribbon in her hand that, at this time last year, would have already been twined around evergreen boughs draped around the entire barn. Last December, Jackson and his father would have been well on their way to having most of the decorations up. Except for the sprig of mistletoe hung over the makeshift dance floor.

Dad used to save the placement of the mistletoe for last, and the preserved bunch of leaves and berries had been the final decoration he took down after each festival. Only last year, he'd barely had the chance before he succumbed to the seizing pain in his chest. By then there had been no hope of saving him.

Jackson would forever regret not insisting his father seek medical attention earlier that night. Jackson had known something had been wrong; the way his father had been sweating as they cleaned up the barn and put away the decorations, his unusual pallor throughout the festival…

Lori cleared her throat. "Precisely why they need the kind of break the festival would give them."

Jackson ran a work-roughened hand over his face. She still didn't get it. *He* was barely hanging on. How could she expect everyone else to hold their lives together if she added more to their plates?

He forced himself to move farther into the barn. "I said no, Lori. The festival isn't going to happen this year."

She shot a glance at his mother. "What about just the pot-luck dinner and dance here in the barn?"

He shook his head at her tenacity. Doing his damnedest to keep his gaze off the boxes of Christmas decorations, he walked toward one of the back corners where he suspected a couple of old shovels might be stored. "No. A potluck means cooking. Seeing as not everyone has their water back on, I don't imagine trying to cook more than is necessary to feed their own would be much fun. Not to mention the man-hours to turn this barn into a place where people would want to eat and dance."

He and his dad used to do the cleanup and most of the decorating, but when time was tight due to bad weather or other delays, they could always count on as many of their neighbors as needed to come and help get the job done.

From behind him Lori said, "Since Grandpa is being stubborn about what he'll let me do for him, I'm sure I can make time to take care of everything here in the barn."

Jackson snorted and stepped around a stack of grain sacks. He spotted the shovels exactly where he'd hoped they'd be. "There's no way you could do it all. And if you have that much time to kill, we could use another young healthy back in a certain ditch with a shovel."

"You have no idea what I'm capable of doing now, Jackson," she called.

"That's right, Lori. I don't." And she knew exactly why. But he'd give up on this town before he let her know how much her leaving had cost him.

He grabbed the three old shovels, even though one was more suited for gravel than dirt. The sooner he got himself out of this barn and away from all the barbed memories, the better.

Lori retorted, "Just as you clearly have no idea what the people of Hooper Creek are capable of. And you won't until you give them the chance to prove it."

He came back around the stack of grain, intending to remind her that she hadn't been around to see what they'd proved themselves capable of.

"Lori's right, Jackson." His mom's soft voice stopped him cold. Her attention was on the very sprig of mistletoe he'd thought about a moment ago. She held it in one hand while she gently touched the bunches of white berries and straightened the green velvet bow with the other.

He couldn't believe she could possibly feel differently about any part of the Christmas festival than he did. So why was she standing there with Lori?

Despite the dread erupting in his stomach, he asked, "About what?"

"Our neighbors, the dance and potluck…" She held the mistletoe high to admire it, her mouth curling upward in a small, sad smile that tore at Jackson's heart.

"Mom—"

"This town—" She looked at him, her hazel eyes shimmering in the light coming through the barn's windows. "You and I need at least this part of the festival. We can't abandon something so important. Not this year."

He wanted to shout, *Yes, we can. Especially this year.* Instead he headed for the door, unwilling to haggle over a done deal. "I've already said no."

His mom waited for him to storm past her, then calmly said, "And I'm saying yes."

Jackson's blood turned to ice even as his mind insisted he'd misheard. His mom wouldn't do this to him.

He turned slowly to face her. When her sad eyes met his, she continued. "I love you and will always need you, but as long as I'm still around, technically this barn is mine. I hate to do this to you, sweetheart, but I'm pulling rank. I want Lori to put on the potluck dinner and dance, here in this barn, using these decorations." She gestured with the sprig of mistletoe. "It's what your dad would have wanted."

As if he'd just witnessed his father crumpling to the ground all over again, Jackson couldn't breathe. Going ahead with at least part of the festival might have been what his dad would have wanted, but next to Lori Whittaker's unexpected return, his mother's ultimatum—tantamount to betrayal—was the last thing in the world Jackson needed.

So he did the only thing he could; he tugged at the bill of his cowboy hat and forced out the words. "Good luck with that, then."

And turned and walked away.

Chapter Three

An hour later, Lori stopped at the very lip of the deep, roughly forty-foot-long trench that had been Mesa Street. She eyed the men toiling away at the arduous job of exposing enough of the broken water main so it could be quickly repaired by the county.

To keep from further damaging the huge pipe on either side of the breaks, they had to remove the water-saturated earth with shovels, then dump it into buckets. The buckets were then hauled up with ropes by what looked to be members of the high school football team. Clearly backbreaking work for all.

But Lori was up for it, infused with an energy born of purpose and an unwavering determination to show Jackson what she was made of. Enthusiastically outfitted by her grandpa in his green hip waders, yellow rain slicker and heavy work gloves, she was ready to prove herself to one Jackson Hooper. She'd even brought her own shovel.

Her gaze automatically sought out Jackson's broad back, immediately recognizable despite the fact he'd exchanged his brown cowboy hat for a well-worn baseball cap and was one of a dozen men bent over in the trench. Her breath caught in her throat at the sheer capable, masculine beauty of him, mud and all.

Although it would have protected his upper half from being

coated in the slimy mud, he'd already shed his dark green rain slicker and was working in a T-shirt that would never be white again. At least he still had on the bottom half of his rain gear, held up by suspenders that accentuated the breadth of his strong shoulders.

He had such presence. Jackson was a natural leader among these independent-minded men—mostly because in between his deeply intoned instruction, he dug the hardest and the fastest. He earned the men's respect.

He certainly had hers, and for far more grown-up reasons than when they'd been together ten years ago. She'd admired his looks and humor back then. Now she saw something much more compelling in him, a steady strength she wanted to reach out to and hold tight.

If she tried, he'd step away.

Her heart twisted in her chest. She had some respect of her own to earn.

Especially after his mother had sided with her an hour ago in the Hoopers' barn. The horror and disbelief that flashed across his handsome face before he'd shuttered it and simply turned and walked away had rocked Lori back on her heels. Not only because hurting him caused her as much grief as it did him, but because his last words and his abrupt departure had been so similar to what he'd done after she'd told him she was considering leaving Hooper Creek ten years ago.

Had a similar expression of pain crossed his face then?

She would never know, because she'd been staring down at her hands gripped in her lap, too immature to look him in the eye when she dropped her bomb. Secretly, deep beneath all her other rationalizations, she'd hoped he'd fight for them.

He hadn't, so she'd left.

Had she read him wrong?

Lori shook off the question. Whether or not she'd been

wrong about how Jackson had felt about her back then was a moot point, because there was no doubting how he felt now.

She did doubt his estimation of what the people of Hooper Creek were capable of. Only she'd matured enough in the past decade to not trust her assumptions any more than she trusted others'. She'd find out for herself what she could ask of the townsfolk before enlisting the necessary help for decorating the barn.

She pulled in a breath for courage, struck a pose with her shovel held out at arm's length and called down into the trench, "One young, strong back reporting for duty, Mr. Hooper!"

Jackson lurched upright and turned to look up at her, along with every other man in the trench. His was the only face not to split wide with a surprised but welcoming smile.

Before he had a chance to say anything—assuming he would have, and she wasn't so sure—several of the men shouted up at her.

Darrell Swanson yelled, "Hey, Lori Beth! Does your grandpa know how to raise 'em right, or what? Get on down here, girl, and pretty up the scenery."

Jeff Hadridson said, "Think long and hard before you do, darlin'. It stinks something awful in this pit, and I'm not talking about the mud."

Lori smiled cheekily down at him. "Clearly you've forgotten about the hog I raised that took blue ribbons across three counties, Mr. Hadridson." She waved her hand in front of her nose. "Talk about stink!"

Mr. Nelson, a tall, slender man who owned the town's general store, pointed up at her and grinned. "I remember that pig. You were itty-bitty and it was huge. Would have gone for a wad of money at auction if you'd have allowed it to be slaughtered."

His son and near mirror image, Travis, whom she'd grown up with, added with a dismissive wave softened by a wink, "She wouldn't even let us ride it."

She wiggled her fingers at him. "Because you insisted on wearing those spurs you got one Christmas all the time, Trav."

His dad propped an elbow on his shovel and asked, "Blue-bell, wasn't it?"

Mr. Swanson guffawed and sunk his shovel into the mud. "No, that wasn't the porker's name. Your memory is as fresh as your produce, Art. She named the monster Rosebud."

Warmed to the depths of her soul by these guys' memories of her, no matter how faulty, Lori laughed. Best of all, none of the men appeared to be on the brink of spirit-breaking exhaustion. How could Jackson be so far off the mark about them?

"Its name was Buttercup," Jackson corrected in a tone that put a quick end to the banter as he stepped onto the pipe and jumped to the side of the trench directly beneath Lori. "What are you doing here?"

She stared down at him. "You remember my pig's name?"

"I remember everything about you, Lori," he stated matter-of-factly.

Though she was stunned, her pleasure increased tenfold.

"Why aren't you still unpacking decorations?"

Was that a glimmer of hope in his green eyes? Did he think she and his mother had changed their minds about holding part of the festival? Or was it resignation because he knew her well enough not to hope?

She cleared her throat. "I decided I'd better come help with this first. Because you're at least right about cooking with no water not being fun."

"At least." He snorted and jammed the toe of his work boot into the mud. "Well, I'm not sure you'll be much help. This ground is so saturated, it weighs a ton. Literally." He started to turn away, obviously dismissing her offer to help.

His rejection stung.

Everyone had heard their exchange, including Mr. Swanson, who said, "She's small enough to get between the pipe and the shoring on the trench wall on that right side." He pointed to what he was talking about. "If she can get the mud cleared away by even a foot, we won't have to take apart the boards securing that side and bring in the backhoe again. Save us a day, minimum, and we won't have to worry about not being ready for the county crew when they're ready for us."

Jackson planted a hand low on his hip and considered the narrow space Mr. Swanson was talking about, then looked back up at her.

Even though she knew his thoughts weren't pleasant, her skin tingled. Jackson Hooper had been her first. She was struck just then by how content she'd be if he were her last. She'd have to get him to stop hating her before she could even think about that.

His eyes locked on hers and narrowed. "You sure you're up to this?"

She ignored her physical response to him because it would only get in the way of what she wanted to accomplish here. "I was serious when I said I've come back to help."

He accepted her pronouncement with an abrupt nod. "Okay."

He reached up a hand. Lori bent and took it, her heart rate picking up over nothing more than his strong fingers closing around hers. He helped her down the steep, slimy side of the trench with tremendous care, drawing enough smiles and nods of approval from the other men that her cheeks blazed with heat by the time she reached the pipe.

Her composure wasn't helped by the fact that the second Jackson let go of her, she lost her footing and almost fell on her butt. He caught her by the elbow with his free hand, then wisely held on. Always the gentleman, this one. He had to know the kind of sexual power he wielded.

Jackson guided her to the place where the side of the trench was vertical enough that a wooden wall had been erected to protect against a collapse. Mr. Swanson was right; a grown man couldn't fit in the space left between the wall and the pipe. She obviously could. The fact that she was needed here filled her with satisfaction in a way her job with the airline never had.

Pointing with his broad, flat shovel, Jackson said, "Do you see that crack in the ductile iron? We have to expose enough of the pipe beyond the crack that we can be certain the county can make a clean repair. It'd be great if you could squeeze in there where we can't reach and scrape the earth away. But here—" He handed her his shovel, one that he'd taken from the barn earlier. "Use this one with the shorter handle."

She traded shovels with him. "I'll do my best, Jackson."

His gaze caught and held hers. "I know. And thank you for being willing to do this."

There were so many memories in his eyes, so many places she wanted to visit again to find out if she had indeed been a fool to leave. She opened her mouth to say she was sorry about what had happened in the barn. But now was not the place.

Travis confirmed it by shouting, "Hey, no making out in the trench. Save it for the dance floor."

Jackson scowled.

Lori vowed softly, "I didn't say a word to anyone about the festival. And I doubt that your mom would have had a chance to, either. It's just a saying, I'm sure."

With a noise that implied he didn't exactly believe her, Jackson stepped away and said to Travis, "Nah, she's not muddy enough to appeal to me. But you, Darrell—" he pointed at Mr. Swanson, who appeared as if he'd lost his footing more than once in the muck "—you're looking mighty fine."

The trench erupted in laughter and a whole barrage of ribbing and jokes that, thankfully, weren't too off color, undoubtedly out of deference to her.

Lori turned to the task she'd been given and after the second shovelful conceded that Jackson hadn't been exaggerating. The dirt did weigh a ton. She ran on the treadmills and used the strength machines in her apartment building's workout room when she was home, but clearly she wasn't home enough. Within fifteen minutes she was sweating like crazy.

The strenuous demands of the job obviously began to wear on the men, too. Before long, the only talking she heard came from Jackson as he gently gave out instructions that were always tempered with encouragements and heartfelt praise. Heaven help them, this *was* hard work.

And they'd been at this sort of thing for a couple of weeks.

Her willingness to pitch in must have stirred the competitive spirit in some of the other ladies, because soon there were women on the edge of the trench to help haul up the buckets of earth. Or maybe they'd simply finished whatever cleanup job they'd been working on earlier and had trudged on over.

Lori had barely exposed an additional foot of pipe when she came to the conclusion she couldn't expect any of these people to help her decorate the Hoopers' barn. Not because she believed they'd refuse, or that it would be the one last burden to make them decide that living in Hooper Creek wasn't worth it. She couldn't ask them because they deserved the rest.

They would still have the festival she so firmly believed they needed, but she'd be the one doing all the work. The celebration in the Hoopers' barn would be her gift to the town she was only just beginning to understand how much she loved. Just as she was getting a glimmer of how much she'd lost by walking away from Jackson Hooper, maddening though he may be.

JACKSON COULDN'T KEEP his eyes from straying to Lori working valiantly away in her corner. With her part of the trench shored up by a wall he'd built himself, he didn't have to worry about her safety. Which left his mind free to wander to other things.

Boy, was he a liar. He was hopelessly attracted to her. Sweet and clean, or rank with mud—and she now was rank with mud, bless her heart. She'd certainly come into her own. Lori had always been strong, but now she exuded a stubbornness born out of conviction rather than mere bullheadedness.

He knew a thing or two about bullheadedness. While he was unable to do much about her physical draw on him or the admiration he felt for her, he refused to forgive her for convincing his mom to betray him.

Then there was the fact she'd left him.

She was down in this ditch because he'd dared her, plain and simple. Granted, she'd stuck with the digging longer than he'd expected. It had to be close to four o'clock, and she'd shown up not that long after lunch.

He watched her chip away at a hunk of dirt bigger than her head with the tip of her shovel, then with a growl drop the shovel and use her gloved hands to pull the giant dirt clod away from the pipe.

A smile touched Jackson's lips. He empathized with her frustration, but boy, she was cute. Maybe she'd also finally get it through her head that the people of this town were already being pushed to their limits.

Jackson laughed out loud when she kicked the dirt clod after throwing it down. He slogged his way toward her. "Atta girl, Lori. Way to show the dirt who's boss."

She started and grimaced, obviously not expecting an audience. Then she shrugged. "I've learned to get my jollies where I can." Using the back of her glove, she wiped at the sheen of perspiration on her forehead, adding more mud to the smears on her face. Although clearly exhausted, she gamely reached for the shovel.

"Let me." Because he'd been working on cutting the damaged section of pipe away and had lost track of the shovel he'd been using, Jackson took Lori's from her. He scooped up the mound of dirt and dumped it in the bucket she'd been filling. "So there really isn't a steady boyfriend?" *Whoa, where had that come from?* But he guessed the thought of *jollies* automatically led him down the relationship road when it came to Lori.

She blinked at him for a moment in the failing light. The days just weren't long enough in December. At least the poor visibility saved him from her spotting the heat creeping into his cheeks.

Finally she said, "No, there isn't a boyfriend. How did you know?"

He mimicked her shrug and speared another hunk of dirt. "My mom talks to your grandpa all the time. Then she, of course, talks to me. But since there's always the chance of creative interpretation, I thought I'd ask for myself."

He'd often wondered if his mother kept him apprised of Lori's romantic life in the hope that one of these days he'd finally bite the bullet and go after her. Only to be told she still wasn't the slightest bit interested in the life he'd been destined—or maybe some like Lori would think doomed—to live here in Hooper Creek? No, thank you.

Lori nodded in understanding of his explanation. "Small town."

"Yep, small town." He dumped the shovelful in the bucket, realizing he'd opened a door between them. Might as well step through. A guy had a right to appease his curiosity, didn't he? "Why?"

Creases formed between her slender eyebrows, making the older, drying mud there crack and flake. "Why?"

Without thinking he propped the shovel handle in the crook of his arm and pulled off a glove to lightly scrape the worst of the dirt flakes away with his fingertip. "Why no boyfriend?"

He couldn't resist trailing his finger down the delicate

bridge of her nose and across her cheek. Her eyelids fluttered shut. His muscles jerked tight in response. Over the years, despite dating a couple of the local women pretty seriously, he'd come to accept that no other woman could bring him to life the way Lori Whittaker had, and the pounding of his blood in his ears confirmed it.

When he pulled his hand back, she opened her eyes and shot him a look he couldn't decipher in the poor light. A stupid part of him began to hope that she was as haunted by their past as he was. Sure, he was capable of loving other women, but none of them tied him up tight then sprung him loose like Lori.

Her scrutiny dropped to her mud-caked, too-big work gloves. "My job has me traveling a lot." She squeezed the empty fingertips of one glove.

"If traveling's a true detriment to romance, then how do baseball players, golfers, national politicians—"

She held up a hand to stop him. "I didn't say I never dated. Just that nothing's…stuck." She picked off a glob of dirt from her forearm. "How about you?"

Her tone sounded casual enough, but the fact she didn't look at him caught his notice. Whatever she might be thinking, though, he wouldn't lie to her. "Let's just say I've been definitely sticky."

Blue eyes jumped to his. *"Sticky?"*

"Yeah, sticky." She'd left. Life had to go on.

Lori nodded slowly, then studied him with an odd light in her eyes. "But not stuck?"

"No, not stuck." So what if he hadn't been willing to put his neck on the chopping block again and wait for the ax to fall? And so what if her interest stirred something crazy in him? "Why hasn't anything stuck for you, Lori?"

She considered her gloves again. "I haven't found what I'd thought I'd find."

Closing himself off to the hurt before she started to describe how he might have been lacking, he finished the thought for her. "Yet."

"Yet."

She was going back to her life in Dallas. The confirmation felt like a shovel connecting unexpectedly with his kidneys. He shouldn't be surprised, but apparently a part of him had started to hope....

Jackson derailed that train of thought and the emotions attached to it. He had no choice but to ignore the yearnings Lori stirred in him. If he couldn't, then he'd have to deal with them the same way he was dealing with the memories the approaching holiday stirred up—by totally avoiding the source.

Chapter Four

Already stiff and sore by that evening, Lori used the shovel as if it were a walking stick to help her climb the two steps to Jackson's front porch, then leaned on it as she knocked on his door.

Okay, returning the shovel Jackson had lent her was an excuse to come see him tonight. But she wanted the chance to talk to him alone about the compromise she'd decided on while down in the ditch—that they would hold the potluck dinner and dance in his family's barn, only she would do the decorating herself. And after he'd shown an interest in her love life, albeit casual, she'd begun to hope that maybe more than the water main could be mended around here. So she had fixed her grandpa a casserole, and hopped in her car.

Unfortunately, her nerves had decided to go on a rampage the moment she'd steered her red Subaru Forester around the north pond. It was a tidy oiled-gravel drive, that had once been nothing more than a cow trail and Jackson's two-story home soon came into view.

He'd built it without cutting down the old oak they'd spent hours sitting under, instead tucking the roof of the wraparound porch beneath the tree's canopy as if house and tree had grown up together. When she'd approached the porch, an odd, prickling sensation had started on the back of her neck, joining in with the nervous tumble in her stomach.

Maybe because there wasn't a holiday decoration in sight. No wreath, lights, nothing. Very, very un-Hooper-like.

The large but almost cabinlike house was extremely masculine, rustically finished with a dark stain that furthered the impression of cohesion with the tree. She shifted her attention to the two Adirondack chairs on the porch. Much more appropriate to Jackson's size and personality than the rockers or swing on his mother's porch.

Who joined him to watch the sun glint off the pond on a lazy summer evening? Who did he *get sticky* with out here? Heartache and longing seeped through her, compromising her emotional strength just as the flood had compromised so many buildings in Hooper Creek.

Unlike Jackson's mother, her grandfather had been remiss in keeping her up-to-date on Jackson's romantic liaisons. She racked her brain for who among the ladies in the area might be single, either still or again, but the door swung open and she was greeted by the sight of Jackson's bare chest.

Her mind went utterly blank, then as quickly filled with signals from pretty much every female part of her. And she became very aware of the snug fit of her light blue fleece pullover top and her well-worn jeans.

Goodness, but he *had* filled out since she'd seen him last. With nothing but muscle. His shoulders, his pecs, his stomach, were all well defined and rock solid. If she'd needed proof of how hard he'd been working since the flood, he'd just given it to her.

She blurted, "Jeez, Jackson, you're *ripped.*"

An eyebrow twitched upward. He stared at her for a moment. "And you should be home in bed. Or at the very least, soaking in a tub," he replied almost testily, shoving a hand through his wet hair. He must have finished showering only moments ago.

A flush of embarrassment spread up her neck. There'd

been a time when her unguarded comment would have been greeted with a slow, sexy smile and a return compliment that usually led to more physical demonstrations of appreciation. Often under this very tree. Those days were apparently over.

Although she could swear a hint of pink was also spreading just beneath the tanned skin of his cheeks. But if her comment and his reaction to it made him mad, then what she thought of him didn't matter. Maybe nothing she did would matter to him ever again.

She thrust the shovel at him. "I'm returning your shovel."

He propped the handle against the wall. "It could have waited."

He was right, so she came clean. "And I want to talk to you about what I decided today."

"Which is?"

"Can I come in?"

He hesitated, and his obvious reluctance to allow her into his home stung. The fledgling hope she'd held for them curled up and died. But before she could turn to leave, he relented with a grunt and moved back, waving her inside.

Lori took two steps beyond the threshold and stopped dead at the sight of the interior of Jackson's house. He had to nudge her aside to close the door.

At first, she thought she must be imagining things, but after a moment, the threat of tears burned in her eyes and she couldn't take in anything more than shallow breaths as the hope for a future with Jackson she was just about to bury jumped back to life.

With shocked wonder she said, "You built it."

He stalked past her, his bare feet silent on the light oak flooring, and disappeared around the two-story, free-standing natural stone fireplace that served as the centerpiece to the large, open living area. Plump brown leather furniture faced an entertainment unit that held a big-screen TV and stereo system on the wall to her right, and a long, antique dining room table with seating for eight filled the space to her left. The rooms upstairs opened to an oak-railed balcony that ringed the great room on three sides, with nothing above the entryway.

The house was just as she'd described it to him all those years ago.

His mother's words danced through Lori's brain. *I would have thought you'd known since Jackson started planning his house long before you left for Dallas.*

A clothes dryer door opened and slammed shut.

Her heart racing, Lori moved forward until she could see around the fireplace to the big kitchen and breakfast nook. "You built my dream house, Jackson," she called.

A black shirt in his hands, Jackson reappeared from a short hallway between the kitchen and the base of the staircase, which hugged the wall on its way up to the second story. Below the stairs, a beautifully carved, dark wooden desk faced the fireplace, with matching shelves and credenza filling the corner.

"It's just a house," he practically growled. He shook out the button-down shirt with a crisp *snap* and shoved his arm into a sleeve.

"No it's not. It's my fantasy house. The house I told you about on this very spot beneath that old tree!" She emphasized the last words with a jab of her finger in the direction of the huge oak tree outside.

He shrugged her words off and his shirt on. "So it was a good fantasy. Big deal."

Patsy had told her he'd built a house, but the fact he'd built *this* house, on *this* spot, *was* a big deal, and his behavior and stiff tone confirmed as much. Even after she'd left, he'd made a dream of hers a reality.

And hadn't wanted her to know it. Hurt trickled through her. So much for *build it, and she'll come.*

Shirt hanging open, Jackson planted his hands low on his hips. "What did you want to talk to me about, Lori?"

Sorely distracted by her discovery—not to mention the swath of tan skin and rippling muscles left exposed by his open shirt—she had to think for a moment. "Oh! The festival. I've decided you're right."

His hands dropped to his sides. "You—" He started toward her, his forehead furrowed in concern. "Did you drink any water while you were digging?"

She rolled her eyes at the insinuation that dehydration was affecting her thinking. When he reached her he pushed her hair back and gently held her head, his gaze touching upon every inch of her face. His expression changed from concern to something softer, more promising. He'd tried to hide it, yet it was there. Jackson had cared for her far more than she'd known.

His nearness, the heat coming off his big body, his touch, this house, *everything* conspired to steal the bones from her body and intelligent thought from her head.

His fingers moved in her hair. "I'm glad you finally realized the festival—any part of it—is just too much right now."

To keep from getting completely lost in the fields of his eyes, she lowered her attention to his mouth. And wanted nothing more than to kiss him and make love to him under the old oak tree as if the past ten years had never happened. But they had, and he deserved the clarification she'd never given him.

She settled her hand between his open shirt on the warm, bare skin at the base of his sternum. Instead of urging him back, her fingers flexed of their own volition. Jackson's muscles jumped beneath her touch and knocked her resolve completely off kilter. She shifted toward him, just a little, but enough to bring her lower belly in contact with the wash-worn, buttoned front of his jeans. Her insides turned molten and desire for him gripped her hard.

Jackson didn't move, his breathing shallow and pensive. But no matter how much she wanted to, she couldn't start something with him until he knew the truth about her plans.

Closing her eyes against temptation, she whispered, "The dance is still going to happen, Jackson. What you were right about was the fact that I can't ask for help decorating and readying the barn. And no one will be expected to bring food."

Jackson eased back from her, leaving nothing but static-laden air beneath her palm and an ache in her heart.

When he spoke, his voice was cold and edged with bitterness. "I should have known that even delirium couldn't get you to budge over something you've set your mind to. You haven't changed a bit, Lori Beth."

He might as well have smacked her. Her eyes snapped open and she made a fist of her hand, bringing it against her own chest to press against the frustration burning there. "Yes I have, Jackson. And if *you'd* stop being so stubborn you'd see it."

A muted scratching and whining at a door came from behind him. Scowling at her as he buttoned his shirt, Jackson turned and went back down the hall. A door opened and closed, and the clicking of nails on the hardwood heralded the arrival of a barrel-chested golden Labrador retriever. The dog spotted Lori and came straight for her to be petted, tail wagging and tongue lolling.

"Well, hello," she greeted the dog, smoothing a hand over its broad, silky head.

"That's Rio."

She scratched behind the dog's ear. "I'm surprised his name isn't Max."

"Max? Why Max?"

She glanced around the holiday-decoration-free house, then sent Jackson a pointed look. "Like the Grinch's dog? You know, in Dr. Seuss's *How the Grinch Stole Christmas?*" To the dog she said, "Where are your fake antlers, boy?"

Jackson snorted. "Very funny." Turning, he headed for the kitchen. "Now, assuming you've said what you came to say…" He raised a hand toward the front door. "I haven't eaten yet, and I'm starved."

Rebelling against the thought of being so blithely dismissed from his life, especially now after learning the extent to which he'd cared for her, she followed him instead. "So am I. What do ya got?"

He stopped and stared at her. "You expect me to feed you?"

"I expect you to be the gentleman I know your mother raised."

He sighed, then turned and grumbled something rude on his way to the refrigerator.

Lori smiled despite herself. The man was adorable. Maddening, but adorable. He proved it further by proceeding to lay out a veritable feast for her, cobbled together from the contents of his fridge. Rio scored a cup of premium dried dog food in his dish at the base of the counter.

Seated at the small, round table tucked into the far windowed corner of the kitchen, she nibbled on a piece of roast beef left over from a previous night's meal. "This is delicious, Jackson. Leftovers from Sunday night dinner at your mom's?"

He finally sat down with a groan of exhaustion in the chair opposite her. "Mine."

Lori's jaw went slack. "You cooked this?"

"Being a grown man, and all. Yes, I can cook. And I'm a demon with a Crock-Pot." He stabbed a slice of beef and started to build a sandwich out of a sourdough roll.

She laughed. "A demon, eh?"

"Yep. Give me a big ol' electric Crock-Pot—" he jerked a thumb toward the counter where indeed sat a big ol' brown and gold electric crock pot "—any kind of meat and vegetables, some onion soup mix or chicken broth, garlic or other spices, and *voilà*." He waved a hand over the roast beef.

Realizing this was the perfect opportunity to bridge at least some of the barriers between them, those created by distance and the passage of time, and get to know each other again, she offered, "I don't cook much. Seems silly to buy groceries when I'm gone so often."

She shook her head in wry amusement. "I'll never forget the time I had to go on the road for three weeks for work and left an eggplant in the fridge. Talk about a science experiment."

The next thing she knew, they were sharing stories of their lives, giving glimpses of the people they'd become over the past decade. She discovered he'd seriously dated both Terra Cannel and Stacy Gustavson but, for a reason he would only shrug off, hadn't gotten around to taking the next step to commitment with either one of them, and the relationships had fizzled.

Whether or not Jackson picked up on how unhappy she was with her life she couldn't tell, but she certainly picked up on the hint of loneliness in his routine despite having his mom and so many friends and at least two women close at hand.

Hers to own or not, the weight of responsibility nearly crushed her, and Lori was seized by a need to make him understand the choices she'd made back then.

She slid her hand across the table and covered his where it rested next to his empty plate. "I was wrong to leave, Jackson."

He stilled, studying her hand.

She rushed on before she lost her nerve. "But back then I thought I owed it to my parents to at least see if life had more to offer me than what I could find in Hooper Creek."

That brought his head up. "Your *parents?* You never said a word—" He shook his head, cutting himself off. "I hadn't even known you'd been sending out job applications. I'd always assumed you were planning to put your business management degree to use here at the ranch."

"I didn't send out applications. I only attended a job fair

my last quarter at school out of curiosity, to see if there was more to life—"

"I'm sorry I left you so unfulfilled, Lori Be—"

"No. Don't. Please, just listen. It wasn't about you. I did what I thought my parents would have wanted me to do. Truth be told, I was wrong to think what I did. I see that now. The way of life, the traditions, *everything* I've come to realize is important to me is right here."

With you.

She squeezed his hand, but the coward in her added, "In Hooper Creek. Can you ever forgive me?"

He pulled his hand from beneath hers. "Truth be told? No, Lori, I can't. You eviscerated me that day."

She gaped at him, her throat tight and her eyes burning. "You didn't tell me. You never asked me to help you with the ranch. You never told me how much you cared. You *never said the words,* Jackson. How was I supposed to know? I'm not some sort of mind reader."

"I thought I'd *showed* you. Besides, I wasn't going to beg you not to leave. If you'd loved me enough, you would have stayed."

Pushing his chair away from the table, he stood. "And it just hit me how damn tired I am. I'm going to bed. You know the way out." He turned and walked away with his dog at his heels, leaving Lori staring after him, horrified.

A door slammed shut upstairs, jolting her out of her stupor. A blessed numbness stole over her. Slowly she rose from the table and began clearing the dishes and putting away the remaining food.

She'd learned a lot today. Not only had Jackson cared more for her, far more, than she'd known, but she'd hurt him far deeper, too.

BY THE NEXT WEEK, Jackson had come to the conclusion that not only was he a liar, but he was a fool, to boot.

He stepped back into the shadows outside the barn window. He'd been watching Lori through it as she worked at decorating inside and now he leaned a shoulder against the coarse wood planking of the barn wall. The defeated slump of her slender shoulders beneath her gray thermal shirt and blue quilted vest cut him to the bone.

He should have never come down here.

Regardless of his best intentions to avoid her, all he'd been able to think about on his way home after he'd seen Lori driving the tractor—a huge noble fir tree, harvested from the small stand his father had planted on their property for that exact purpose, dragging along behind—was that she could get hurt. Hoisting a tree that size was without a doubt a two-man job, at the very least. The thing could easily crush her.

Even if she gave up on the tree, he'd had visions of her falling from the ladder while stringing garlands and lights on the rafters or, worse yet, while hanging that damn mistletoe.

So after showering off the skin-stiffening mud from the water-main ditch and dressing in clean jeans and sweatshirt, he'd hustled down to the barn to keep an eye on her. Surreptitiously, of course. How lame was that?

Shoving a hand into his damp hair, he looked back through the window. He just couldn't handle walking in there with even a few of the decorations up. From what he could see through the dirt-smudged glass, Lori had already accomplished a lot before she'd brought in the tree.

His dad's yards and yards of artificial evergreen garlands, wrapped with twinkling white lights, were draped around the barn and beneath the ceiling beams, hung from hooks left year-round. She'd set up the tables along the walls, ready for holiday dishes his mom and her friends were preparing.

Normally those tables would have been stored in the rafters, but last year he hadn't had the emotional or physical energy to put them away properly, and he had simply stacked them in the back of the barn. She wouldn't have been able to get them down otherwise.

Aside from the tree, everything looked pretty much as it should the night before the culmination of the Hooper Creek Christmas festival.

Walking into this barn would be like walking into his worst recurring nightmare.

He looked up to the center beam above her. The only saving grace would be that she hadn't hung the mistletoe.

He planted a hand on the windowsill and leaned his weight against it. If only he could turn his back on all of this.

On her.

But the sight of her sitting on her heels, her knees on the freshly swept floor, her hands limp in her lap and her head bowed next to the tree she wasn't strong enough to lift upright tore at him like nothing else.

Having her in his house last week, seeing the truth of his feelings for her dawn in her eyes, followed as dramatically by regret, made all his denials that he couldn't forgive her ring false.

It was time to face the truth.

He shoved off from the barn window and watched Lori push to her feet, turn and walk out of his sight, her head still down. The interior of the barn went dark.

Jackson started for the front of the barn, dodging a pile of lumber and stacks of hay Lori must have moved to clear space for the festivities. She *had* accomplished a lot. The lady sure knocked his hat back.

But before he could round the corner of the barn, he heard a car door slam shut and the engine rev to life. He reached the circle of light created by the big halogen lamp mounted high above the barn doors just as Lori put her red SUV in gear and drove away, freshly laid gravel flying from beneath her tires.

Damn. He'd hesitated too long. However, unlike with his father's death, Jackson could *do* something about the pain

Lori's upset was causing him. But did he have the emotional strength? So far, the answer had been a resounding *no*. Could he do it now?

Unfortunately, there was only one way to find out.

Chapter Five

Lori cursed under her breath when the tow chain wouldn't release from around the trunk of the second noble fir tree she'd cut down in as many days. But the stubbornness that had sent her back out to the Hoopers' ranch this morning after all but giving up the night before made her yank on the chain with her gloved hands until the snagged links came free.

She would not fail the town. They needed traditions to cling to right now. *She* needed traditions. A sob caught in her throat. She'd tossed and turned all night trying to decide if she was indeed brave enough to stay here in Hooper Creek knowing Jackson would never want her again.

Maybe, with time, she could prove to him whatever it was he needed her to prove. Maybe not. She'd finally decided to give herself until after Christmas to make up her mind about staying.

Her physical exhaustion was nothing compared to how emotionally drained she felt. Nonetheless, she grasped the tree trunk in one hand and dragged the tree behind her to the barn doors. At least she'd remembered to close the doors when she left last night. Not returning the tractor to the equipment shed had been bad enough.

Hopefully Patsy hadn't minded. Jackson's mother had been in such a baking frenzy in preparation for the potluck tonight, she might not have noticed. Especially because when word spread around town—probably via Grandpa—that Lori and Patsy were putting on the dance and potluck, Mrs. Perez and a couple other ladies had insisted on coming to help out in the Hoopers' kitchen. Judging from the amount of laughter last night, the old gals might have been doing a little pre-celebrating.

Lori let go of the trunk, shoved the double doors wide, then pulled the tree into the gloom. She glanced at one set of dirt-glazed windows that graced both sides of the barn. While their condition wouldn't really matter after dark when the party was scheduled, pride compelled her to wash them sometime today. If she turned out to be lucky for once, she'd have time.

A spark of reflected light at the back of the barn caught her attention. She stopped and stared, trying to make sense of what she was seeing. Her fingers suddenly numb, she dropped the tree trunk and eased forward. The tall mass at the back of the cavernous space slowly took shape.

With a gasp, she ran to switch on the lights.

The tree she'd so optimistically cut down and hauled here yesterday, only to be so soundly defeated by its size, was no longer ignominiously lying on the floor where she'd left it. And the noble fir was no longer a mere tree, planted and lovingly tended for years by Jackson's father.

Standing straight in a huge stand, the tree had been transformed into a picture-perfect Christmas miracle with lights, glass balls in every color imaginable, gold bead garlands and starched crocheted snowflakes made by Patsy and her friends over the years.

A glorious memory from Lori's childhood come to life.

She cried out and covered her mouth.

Only Jackson could have done this. She'd emphatically told any who inquired that she had the barn decorating handled to the point that she'd be locking the doors, and Patsy—

the only person other than Jackson who might have discovered otherwise last night—couldn't have managed this much decorating any more than Lori could have. Although, how Jackson had accomplished raising the tree by himself was beyond her.

Clearly, he had changed his mind about this part of the festival.

Her heart pounded and hope surged. Could he have changed his mind about forgiving her, also?

She looked up, high above to the barn's center beam. He'd hung the mistletoe.

Joy engulfed her at the mere possibility that he'd forgiven her, coupled with the proof before her of his changing his mind about the festival. She spun and ran for the doors, planning to sprint up the hill to Jackson's house to thank him for spending what had to have been the majority of the night putting up and decorating the tree for her.

The thought of him being up all night brought her to a screeching stop. If he'd been up all night, odds were good he was still asleep. In bed. Probably wearing nothing more than a pair of checked cotton boxers, the bedding tossed to one side as he slept. The image sent her own temperature skyrocketing.

She could walk right through his undoubtedly unlocked front door and go straight to his room. Then she could touch more of that skin and muscle she hadn't been able to stop thinking about since being at his house. Maybe waking him by kissing her way up—or down—his amazing chest and stomach. She could certainly do a little *showing* of her own.

No. What they needed was what they'd needed back then— to talk. And even if she were able to resist the temptation of Jackson in bed and rouse him by banging on his door, he needed the sleep. She'd wait until he appeared on his own accord and thank him—*profusely*—then.

There were still plenty of minor details to see to: tablecloths and centerpieces, collecting favorite music CDs and tapes to play on the portable stereo Travis had loaned her, and one final sweeping of the floor. Heck, she definitely had time to wash the windows now. Maybe she could decorate the outside of the barn, too. There were more than enough strands of lights to do the job.

God willing, the residents of Hooper Creek would come tonight, and for the first time in weeks, forget about their worries and the hardships they faced and spend a few hours having fun and enjoying the season as they had in years past.

Riding a cloud of euphoria, Lori threw herself into her work. When Jackson still hadn't appeared by lunchtime, she convinced herself he'd gone back to work on the water main. She had simply missed seeing him drive by on his way out to the road. He might even be suffering from a touch of embarrassment for putting up such a stink about the festival for so long.

Tonight, maybe under the mistletoe, she would tell him it was all right, and hopefully he would forgive her for her transgressions, too.

The image of her in Jackson's arms beneath the mistletoe blazing in her head and heart, she left the barn at four-thirty for her grandpa's. She showered and changed into her red cowboy boots, a long denim skirt and a Christmas sweater with a tree that bore a striking resemblance to the one Jackson had decorated.

Grandpa laughed off her gentle urgings to hurry, but still managed to clean up and change in record time into a merino wool turtleneck and cords she'd given him for his birthday. The rubber boots he stomped into on the porch made her vision swim and her heart swell. This was going to be the best night of her life.

By the time they reached the Circle H barn, several trucks were already parked in the graveled area out front. She knew it! Hooper Creek did need this. Tradition might not completely heal the wounds left by the flood, but there was nothing wrong with a little soothing.

People continued to arrive until the barn was as full as she remembered it being in the best of times. Seemingly everyone was there.

Everyone but Jackson.

THE OILED GRAVEL CRUNCHED beneath Lori's cowboy boots as she stomped her way in the dark toward Jackson's house with Rio at her side. The party was still in full swing in the barn behind her, with Travis trying to teach Grandpa and Patsy the latest line dance while Darrell did his best to single-handedly eat all the cookies the ladies had baked. All in all, the sense of renewed hope among those in attendance was palpable, which made it all the more obvious who was absent. Jackson's dog had shown up outside the big double doors not long after eight, happily greeting everyone, but by almost eleven o'-clock, it'd become clear to her that Jackson wasn't coming. If he wasn't home, she'd plant herself on his porch and wait.

She grimly accepted the disappointment of his absence and turned the force of her emotional energy on the questions searing in her mind. This time she wasn't going to make assumptions about Jackson's feelings as she had before. She was going to get some answers out of him, one way or another.

Despite her bravado, a flutter of apprehension moved through her. Was she fully prepared for what those answers might be?

Yes. Because then she'd know.

She was breathing hard by the time she reached his porch, as much from the crushing weight on her chest as from the trek, and her heavy tread was loud against the wooden steps, compared to the faint click of the Lab's nails.

"Need something, Lori?"

She squeaked and jumped at the unexpectedness of Jackson's voice coming from the deeper shadows of the covered porch. Wood creaked and ice tinkled in a glass, and she assumed he was having a drink. He was just sitting there, staring out at the magical scene the decorated barn created below.

His question sank in, and her heart cried, *Yes, you!* Her craving for the truth kept her silent.

Instead, she said, "I need some answers, Jackson Hooper."

"Do you, now?" he drawled.

She marched toward him. "Yes, I do. And I aim to get them tonight."

"Then you'd better have a seat." Wood scraped against wood as he pulled the other Adirondack chair forward. Rio flopped down next to his master.

Lori moved past Jackson and sat down, catching the scent of something familiarly sweet and spicy.

He asked, "You warm enough?"

"I shouldn't be, but I guess I generated enough heat on my way up here."

"Along with a full head of steam, I imagine." He sounded almost amused.

"You could say that. So tell me why you decorated the barn but didn't come to the party, Jackson?"

"Would you like a drink? I have eggnog and spiced rum." He clanked the ice around in his glass. "I can heat it for you, if you'd prefer."

She jerked her hands up in exasperation. "Eggnog? Not only did you somehow raise and decorate that tree down there for me, but you, Mr. Bah Humbug, are sitting here drinking eggnog—"

"Mostly spiced rum."

"—but you didn't come down to the party. Because of me, right?" Her voice cracked. "You didn't want to go because I was there."

"Let's just say I'm a little too emotionally drained to join in the fun."

"Also because of me. I can't blame you for wanting nothing to do with me."

"Oh, sweetheart—" He set his glass down on the porch and his hand found her cheek and rubbed at a tear she hadn't realized she'd shed. "That's not it at all. It's only because of you that I was able to go in there and decorate that tree—after raising it with a rope and pulley system, by the way—and then sit here with eggnog. I couldn't bear to see you so defeated. It tore me up inside. You took off before I could tell you as much."

His hand slipped away. "Funny thing is—" his voice softened "—I went in there for you, but I'm the one who ended up benefiting."

Her heart began to thrum in her ears, and she struggled to keep hope in check. "What do you mean?"

"I'm sure it's no great revelation for me to admit how difficult this Christmas season has been for me."

"You've taken on so much since the flood—"

"No, it has nothing to do with the flood. Make that *floods*. It's because of my dad. I didn't think I could face Christmas without him. And the festival and those decorations… Did you know he had his heart attack while taking down the mistletoe?"

Tears flowed anew. "No. I didn't. No one told me. I'm so sorry, Jackson. I should have never—"

"It's okay, Lori. Really. Just listen to them down there." The sounds of reveling rose up from the barn. "They're having a ball. You were right. There's more to rebuilding a town than hammering and painting."

"But the water thing…"

He laughed. "Yeah, water is kinda critical, but getting the main fixed didn't have to be at the exclusion of everything else. I see that now. Just as I saw that my father can still be with me. He was there when I was putting up the tree you cut. I felt him while I strung the lights and hung the decorations. And I was able to honor him by hanging that mistletoe he loved so much.

"Doing all those things will keep his memory alive for me. Traditions *are* important. You helped me see that, Lori. You helped me own my grief and come to terms with it. You helped me reconnect with my life."

All her fears and anxieties lifted, and for the first time in days she could take a full breath. "I'm so glad, Jackson. The traditions here in Hooper Creek helped me deal with my parents' deaths. And those traditions are part of what was so missing from my life after I left."

The chair creaked as he shifted in it, toward her. "Just part?"

"Yeah." She thought about how fulfilled she'd felt in other ways since returning to her hometown, and how much she wanted to stay for good. "It occurred to me that you helped me see I actually came back to Hooper Creek looking for more than mere tradition."

He scoffed. "When did I do that?"

"When I came to help dig in the water-main ditch. Watching you with everyone… The camaraderie, the caring and fellowship, the *community*. That's also been missing in my life. Ties of the heart are what bring security and contentment, not just traditions."

"Ties of the heart," he mused. "What about trust?"

Lori's throat constricted and she gripped the arm of her chair. Finally they were getting to the crux of the matter. "Trust is important, too. And I know it has to be earned. I swear to you, Jackson, I'll do whatever it takes—however long it takes—to regain your trust, to prove I'll never hurt you again, at least not on purpose. But you have to swear that you'll *tell* me how you feel, what you're thinking and planning, not just *show* me."

His hand sought hers, threading their fingers together. "Showing can be so much fun."

His touch and the gentleness of his voice sent her heart tripping over itself again.

"And I'm kinda good at it." He reached back with his free

hand and rapped on the house. "But because you have a point, I'll also say the words I've come to accept in the past twenty-four hours, though it's not my strong suit." He pulled in a noisy breath. "Apparently my heart will always be tied to you, Lori Beth Whittaker." He said her full name with such love, for the first time in her life it didn't strike her as belittling.

Just the opposite. She felt herself swell with pride and joy and excitement. But most of all, with love.

His voice pitched low with emotion, he continued. "Since you've been back, the knot's gone tight on me. So damn tight. I can't live without you, Lori."

She gasped out a sob and brought their joined hands to her mouth. "I love you, too, Jackson. I love you so much. Even more than before. I was such a fool to leave."

"*Shh,* no," he soothed. "All that matters is that you came back to me, sweetheart. And you wouldn't be the woman you are now if you hadn't left. That's who I want in my life forever. If you're willing."

She laughed through her tears at the absurdity of his doubt. "You'd have a hard time getting rid of me, bucko. After all, you do live in *my* house."

"I do, don't I?" He chuckled, sounding very self-satisfied. Using the hand he held, he pulled her from her chair and onto his lap. "So you'd be interested in becoming an official co-owner by, say, this time next year? My mom would kill us if we didn't give her time to plan and fuss."

"Aren't you the flowery romantic. Be still my heart." An impossibility considering it was about to pound right out of her chest with happiness. "But I'm thinking New Year's Eve next year, instead, so we can start a new tradition."

Jackson released her and found her face with both hands. "A new tradition to go along with our new beginning. I like that. Although…" He slipped one hand from her face and reached into the breast pocket of his quilted shirt coat. "There is something to be said for old traditions." He withdrew a small sprig of mistletoe, barely discernible in the darkness. "This broke off last night, but I figured I could still put it to use."

He did just that, holding it above her head while pulling her mouth down to his. Gripping his shirt in her fists, she opened for him as she had so many years ago under this very tree, only the welcome was heady, more intense. Her entire body throbbed in response. His tongue found hers with a hungry thrust and she rose, lifting herself to press closer against him.

He kissed her long and deep, his mouth melding with hers as if their hearts had never been apart, the mistletoe forgotten as he tangled his fingers in her hair.

Eventually, they both had to come up for air.

Against her lips he whispered, "I love you, Lori. Welcome home."

MERRY TEXMAS
Linda Warren

Dear Reader,

Isn't Christmas a wonderful time of the year? To me it brings back a lot of memories of when I was a kid. We lived in Texas on a farm/ranch and we always cut a cedar tree from the woods. Getting the lights out of the attic was like a treasure hunt. I couldn't wait to see what we'd saved from the year before. We didn't have a lot of money, and icicles and an occasional shiny ornament from Woolworth's were all we could afford. Everything else we tried to make, like a colorful paper chain and strands of popcorn, or my dad's red bandannas tied into bows. Paper angels made in school were my favorite. That's probably where the idea came from for the angels in this story.

Sometimes Christmas is what you make it, and in *Merry Texmas* Chloe Crandall is determined to get her parents, Mariel and Gray, back together. Living on a ranch, Chloe decides they have to make everything for a Texas cowboy Christmas tree. With ornaments of faith, hope and love, Chloe just might get her wish.

Hope you have a little Merry Texmas in your Christmas.

Happy holidays,

Linda Warren

To Paula Eykelhof and Kathleen Scheibling, for allowing me to be a part of this project. And to the other authors, Tina Leonard and Leah Vale—it was a pleasure to get to know you, and it's an honor to share this anthology. Thanks and Merry Christmas. Or should I say Merry Texmas.

Chapter One

Turning twelve sucked. That was Chloe Crandall's opinion.

The old porch swing squeaked as she swayed back and forth with Buffy the cat asleep on her lap. She nervously twisted a strand of blond hair around one finger and chewed on it, half-moon eyes trained on the dirt road that curled to the cattle guard. Watching. Waiting. No sign of a car. Chloe glanced at the new watch her mother had sent for a birthday present. It could tell the time anywhere in the world, but it couldn't tell the time her mother was coming.

That sucked, too.

Yesterday had been Chloe's birthday, and both her parents had missed it again. Her mom, Mariel, was an assistant U.S. Attorney and her father, Grayson, a U.S. Marshal. They both had high-powered, stress-filled jobs. She'd heard that plenty of times. If they were so busy, why did they have a kid, anyway?

She got up and went into the house with Buffy in her arms, and the screen door slammed behind her. Since her parents' divorce, Chloe spend most of the time with her grandmother, Elaine, on a ranch outside Sealy, Texas. Her parents worked in Houston, where Chloe attended a private school during the week. On the weekends, Mariel usually had to go in to her office and brought Chloe to the ranch so she wouldn't be alone at home.

Her mother's condo and her daddy's apartment were like rest stops. Here one week. There the next. She hated being moved around like a parcel with the wrong address. It was time to do something about it. Something she'd heard on the news last week had given her an idea that would make her parents notice her. But did she have the courage to follow through?

"Hi, sweetpea," her grandmother said, looking up from putting a roast in the oven. "Your mom coming?"

"No." Buffy jumped from Chloe's arms and slinked into the kitchen, sniffing the air.

Elaine wiped her hands on a dish towel and hugged Chloe. "She'll be here."

"I suppose," Chloe mumbled into her grandmother's shoulder.

Elaine brushed Chloe's bangs from her eyes. "We need to get your hair cut."

"Mama said she was going to take me."

Chloe had blond hair like her mother and brown eyes like her father. People said she was a combination of the two of them. But neither wanted her. Or at least they didn't want to spend time with her.

"I'm sure she will. I saved the rest of the cake and we'll have another party when she arrives."

The phone rang, so Chloe kept her reply to herself.

"Yes, Mariel," Elaine said into the receiver. "She's right here."

Chloe took the phone, but she already knew what her mother was going to say.

"Hi, sweetheart. I'm so sorry, but I can't get away. This murder trial is running longer than any of us expected. I'll make it up to you. I promise. We'll go shopping, do anything you want."

"Sure, Mama."

"I love you."

"Yeah," Chloe answered, not saying the words back to her mother like she always did. She wasn't feeling very loving.

There was a long pause on the other end of the line. "Chloe, are you okay?"

What would it matter? "Yeah," she said again.

"I'll see you in a couple of days."

"Sure."

Chloe hung up, tears stinging her eyes. She wouldn't cry. Not this time.

MARIEL TODD-CRANDALL laid the phone down, feeling uneasy. Chloe didn't sound like her cheerful, happy self. She'd missed her daughter's birthday again and the guilt weighed heavily upon her. After she and Gray were married, they'd made a conscious decision to have a child, and they'd been delighted when Chloe was born. But in the last few years, they'd both gotten so busy with their jobs, and these days it seemed the two of them had very little time for their daughter. Chloe was spending more and more time with Elaine. It bothered Mariel that someone else was bringing up her daughter. She'd chosen this career, though, and she was doing a terrible job of balancing motherhood and work.

Chloe hadn't said "I love you" and that upset her. They always said that to each other before hanging up—just like she'd always said it to her mom and dad. Tears sprang to her eyes and a suffocating feeling came over her. She fought to breathe. *Not today.* She couldn't handle this today.

She had to call Gray to see if he'd talk to Chloe. As she reached for the phone, her assistant, Evelyn Hale, walked in.

"You're expected back in the courtroom," Evelyn told her.

Mariel replaced the receiver. "I'm on my way."

She'd call Gray later. Despite the problems she and Gray had in their marriage, Mariel was glad they were able to discuss Chloe without any bitterness. Well, some of the time. Then she forced herself to admit the truth—they argued all the time about Chloe. For their daughter's sake, they needed to be able to talk rationally about what was best for Chloe.

She hurried to the courtroom, wondering where Gray was this week. Being a U.S. Marshal meant he traveled a lot—he could be anywhere in the country. Even though her job kept her mind occupied most of the time, Mariel thought about Gray more than she wanted to admit to herself. She missed their talks. She missed a lot of her old life.

At times she felt like a piece of luggage on a conveyer belt, going round and round, with no destination in mind—just waiting for someone.

Waiting for…

The truth slipped through her defenses. Every day she waited for Gray to come back. When the phone rang, her first thought was always of Gray. She'd see a tall, dark-haired man and she'd think it was him. But he wasn't coming back. He'd made that very clear and she only had herself to blame. She was the cause of the breakup of their marriage.

Work obliterated the guilt. But it didn't take away his memory.

CHLOE HEADED FOR HER ROOM when the phone rang again. She grabbed it, hoping her mother had changed her mind. It was her father.

"How's my girl?"

"Fine, Daddy. Are you on the way? We have cake left."

"Oh, baby girl. I'm so sorry. I'm guarding a federal judge and I can't leave just yet. Maybe I'll see you at the end of the week."

"Oh."

"Chloe, I'm sorry."

"I know."

"We'll plan something big—anything you want."

I want you to come see me now.

"Tell Mom to freeze me a piece of that cake. I love you, baby girl."

"Yeah." Chloe hung up.

GRAYSON CRANDALL STARED AT the phone. His daughter hadn't said "I love you." She was usually very affectionate, like his ex-wife. He tended to be more reserved, but he was more open since meeting Mariel. She used to smile all the time—she'd always seemed so happy. That was before the divorce, though. Why hadn't Chloe said the words? She was probably mad at him—she certainly had a right to be.

This wasn't how he'd imagined fatherhood—a long-distance relationship. He'd missed his daughter's birthday again. Damn! He hated how busy he was, but he had a commitment to duty. Still, he had a commitment to Chloe, too.

He wished he'd asked about Mariel, but talking about her wasn't one of his favorite subjects. They'd been so in love, he'd thought their feelings would never die. But at the first sign of trouble in their marriage, that love had faded quickly.

It rankled him that he still woke up reaching for her—every damn morning and every damn night. His finger hesitated over the numbers of his cell phone. They had to talk about Chloe.

Maybe later.

ELAINE STARED AT HER granddaughter. "They're not coming?"

"Nope. Busy. Same old story." Chloe clenched her jaw tight.

"Sweetie—"

"Gran, would you love me no matter what I did?"

Elaine seemed taken aback by the question, but she answered quickly. "Yes, no matter what you did."

"Thank you."

"I'm a bit curious, though. Do you want to share something with me?"

"Not now. I'll tell you later."

Chloe went to her room, opened a drawer and pulled out a beaded purse her mother had given her. Buffy rubbed against her leg and Chloe picked her up and sat on the bed. The cat stretched out on the comforter and watched as Chloe unzipped the purse. Inside was money she'd been saving.

She counted it, but she knew how much was there— $1,114. Her parents were very generous, and she'd been socking the money away for a long time, every birthday, every holiday, every time her dad gave her a twenty to buy what she wanted. She never needed anything, but them.

Until now.

She reached for her journal on the dresser and turned to a new page. She wrote: *The decision.* Closing it, she said to Buffy, "I'll be back later." The cat just tucked her nose between her paws.

Slipping the strap of the purse over her head, Chloe hurried down the hall to the kitchen. "I'll see you later, Gran," she called, going out the back door.

"Where are you going?"

"Over to Colonel Bob's."

"Please don't jump his fences. He doesn't like it when you do that with Flash."

Chloe sighed, not wanting to lie. "It's closer that way. It takes forever to go to the main entrance. I won't hurt anything."

"Chloe—"

She quickly closed the door before Gran could make her promise. At the barn, two dogs ran to greet her. She rubbed their heads. Bogey and Spence were Australian blue heelers, Gran's cow dogs. They were named for some actors that Gran liked, Humphrey Bogart and Spencer Tracy. Chloe had no idea who they were.

She put her thumb and middle finger in her mouth and whistled. Flash, a brown-and-white pinto mare, immediately trotted to the barn. As Chloe slipped a bridle on her horse, Luis, a Mexican who worked for Gran, rode in on a tractor.

"Need help, little one?" Luis asked, jumping down from his seat.

"Nope, got it." She reached for Flash's mane and swung up on her back.

Luis nodded. "Good. We ride bareback in Mexico, makes you good horseman."

"Horsewoman," Chloe corrected.

"*Mucho* good." Luis grinned, revealing a big gap where his front teeth should have been. He was going to get new dentures when he went home to Mexico at Christmas, which wasn't far away.

Chloe rubbed the mare's neck. "She's a fast horse, Luis. Thanks for finding her for me."

"Don't fall off or your Gran'll have my hide."

"No way," Chloe said, and looked at the dogs who gazed up at her eagerly, hoping she was going to herd cattle. "Sorry, boys. Stay," she ordered, then shot out of the barn.

Flash's legs seemed to have wings as they flew over the pastures and cleared the fences enclosing hayfields with ease.

The cool wind stung her cheeks. Chloe loved it here—the freedom, the animals, the fresh air and the sunshine. She never wanted to go back to the city again.

When she reached B & B Thoroughbred Farms, she didn't even slow down. She cleared the white fences as if they were twigs lying on the ground. She halted Flash as they reached the house and racetrack. Colonel Bob, as he was known to everyone, bred racehorses and Chloe loved to come here and watch them run.

The colonel stood by the track talking to his trainer. He was the same age as her grandmother, sixty-six, and that made Colonel Bob an old man, although Chloe didn't think of Gran as old. She still rode a horse every day, but Chloe had never seen the colonel on a horse.

Bob lifted an eyebrow when he saw her. Tall and thin, he always wore his army cap with the pins and medals he'd been awarded while serving in the army. Chloe knew a lot of people were scared of him because of his gruff manner. She got along with him, though, except he kept reprimanding her for jumping his fences and spooking his horses.

Chloe dismounted and led Flash toward him. The trainer returned to the track.

"Chloe, how many times do I have to tell you not to jump my fences?"

"This is important. I need to talk to you."

He shook his head, his medals clinking. "No. You cannot ride my horses."

"Why would I want to ride those old nags?" With her thumb, she gestured toward the track where a rider and the trainer were working with a couple of leggy colts.

"Because you've asked me a number of times," he reminded her.

"Well, I got Flash now and she can outrun any of your horses any day of the week."

Bob snorted. "You got guts, kid. What do you want to talk to me about?"

"It's real important."

"Yes, you've said that. Let's sit over here on the bench beneath this oak."

She tied Flash to a fence and followed him. Sitting beside Colonel Bob, Chloe asked, "You're a divorce attorney, right?"

"Right. Retired colonel and now attorney."

"Gran says you're good 'cause you're a fighter."

"Yes. Have been all my life."

"Do you take cases for kids?"

The eyebrow lifted again. "I'm not aware that any kid needs a divorce lawyer."

"I saw on TV last week that a boy asked to have his father's parental rights terminated. They said he was divorcing his father."

"Yes. I'm aware of the case."

"Would you take a case like that?"

Bob removed his hat, revealing thick white hair. He studied the medals. "Depends on the circumstances."

Chloe looked straight into his eyes. "I want to divorce my parents."

Bob nodded. "Figured we were getting to that."

"How much do you charge? I have money." She lifted her purse to show him.

"Chloe, you can't divorce your parents because they missed your birthday." The colonel had been at her party and knew her parents hadn't showed up.

"It's more than that." She drew a circle with the toe of her boot in the dried winter grass. "I'm shuffled around like something on a sale rack. I'm at Mama's condo then at Daddy's apartment, and I don't like either of those places. They're too cramped and I have nothing to do but watch TV, play on my computer and listen to my stereo. I'm glad they finally agreed to let me stay with Gran when Mama has to work long hours. I love it here. And Gran says I'm not a burden to her."

"Is that how you feel?"

"Yep. Mom and Dad are always trying to fit me into their schedules. If they'd just let Gran have custody of me then they wouldn't have to worry anymore. They wouldn't be arguing all the time and maybe they could be happy again."

"I see. So you want Elaine to have custody?"

"Yep."

"Does she agree with this?"

"I haven't told her yet."

"Mmm." He watched her for a moment. "What will you do if I say no?"

"Hire another attorney. Someone will take my case." She frowned at him. "Are you saying no?"

He grunted. "I know Gray and Mariel. They're good people with very time-consuming jobs."

"I know all that, but if all their time is taken up with their work, I don't understand why they had me in the first place." She kicked at the grass.

"Oh, Chloe, one of these days you'll understand."

"I don't think so. I'm not going back to Houston, to that school or Mama's condo. I'm here for the holidays and I want to stay with Gran all the time, and if you won't help me, I'll find someone who will. I have money."

She jumped up, but Bob caught her arm and pulled her back down. "Sit, young lady. We're not through."

She clamped her jaw tight.

"You need to talk to your parents and tell them what you've told me."

"I have, but they don't listen." A tear trickled out of the corner of her eye and she wanted to wipe it away, but she didn't. She wouldn't cry.

"You're not the only child of divorced parents. A lot of kids are experiencing the same thing that you are."

"Divorce should be outlawed," she said with renewed energy. "If you get married, you should have to stay married, especially if you have kids."

"Hear, hear." Bob nodded.

That sat for a moment in silence.

"Are you going to help me?"

He stared at her face. "You don't have a case. Chloe, I—" He stopped as another tear escaped. "Okay, I'll help you because I think you just want to get your parents' attention, right?"

"It's much more than that," she answered.

"You want to make decisions about your life, but you're a kid and you have to accept the decisions that are made for you. Once we get Gray and Mariel's attention, you have to be ready to accept that, because no court is going to grant you a divorce from them. I don't think you want them completely out of your life, do you?"

As much as she tried to stop it, her bottom lip trembled.

Bob didn't press her. "Once we file a petition, you have to face them. Can you do that?"

She lifted her chin. "Yes."

After a slight pause, he said, "Do you want to take a couple of days and think about this some more?"

"No. I want to do it now." She opened her purse. "How much do you charge?"

"How much do you have?"

"One thousand one hundred and fourteen dollars."

"Good God, Chloe, what are you doing with money like that?"

"My parents want to make sure I have everything I need. It's called guilt money, or that's what I heard Gran call it." She pulled out a wad of bills. "So how much?"

"Put your money away and tell Elaine to put it in the bank or something. You can pay me when this is over."

"Okay," she said, stuffing it back into her purse, "I'll keep it for now. This shouldn't take long, should it?"

"Chloe, it's been my experience to expect the unexpected, so you'd better prepare yourself for the worse possible scenario you can."

"I will, and thank you, Colonel Bob."

"Don't thank me yet. You might feel differently next week."

Chloe didn't think so. She swung onto her horse. "Goodbye."

"Don't jump my—" she heard as she sailed across the white fences to her Gran's place.

Back at the ranch, Chloe removed Flash's bridle and let her loose in the pasture, then ran to her room. Grabbing her journal, she added after the words she'd written earlier:

It's done. I did it. I made a decision to divorce my parents and I don't know if I have enough courage to see it through. Daddy will be angry, but he always seems to be angry. Mama will be hurt and might not say anything. She's quiet a lot. I love my parents, but I don't think they love me anymore. They say they do, but they never make time for me. I want my parents to be happy again, and if they didn't have to worry about me maybe they would be. That's why I have to do this. I want us to be happy again. Colonel Bob said to expect the unexpected. I'm ready.

Chapter Two

Smiling, Mariel stuffed papers into her briefcase. She'd gotten a conviction on the murder trial, adrenaline pumped through her veins. She now had one goal—to leave her office as soon as possible. It was after five and she'd probably be stuck in Houston traffic, but she didn't care. She was finally going to see her daughter.

Evelyn opened the door. "There's a man here to see you."

She'd given her assistant specific instructions that she wasn't seeing anyone else today. "Tell him—"

"Ms. Mariel Todd-Crandall?" A tall man in a suit pushed past Evelyn.

She stood frowning at his arrogance. "Yes."

He handed her some papers and walked out.

"He was very persistent," Evelyn said in her own defense.

"Never mind," Mariel replied. "They're probably some papers from the trial and I really don't have time to go over them."

Evelyn shrugged and left.

Mariel stared at the legal document in her hand. She'd have to wait in traffic, anyway, so she might as well see what this was about.

She gasped as she quickly scanned the papers. Chloe was seeking to have Mariel's parental rights terminated! She sagged against her desk. This couldn't be true. Then she saw the name of the lawyer on the document. Robert Barrett. Grabbing her purse and briefcase, she bolted for the door. She had to get out to the ranch.

GRAY HURRIED INTO HIS apartment, took a quick shower and changed into jeans and well-worn boots. He was going to see his baby girl. It had been almost a month since he'd seen her and he hadn't talked to her in days. When he'd called, she was always out on the ranch. Lately, Chloe hadn't been returning his calls, and what that was about, he wasn't sure. He just wanted to hold his daughter for a while, then they'd go riding. Chloe loved to ride and Gray was proud that she was quite good at it.

As he headed for the door, the buzzer rang. He opened it to a man he'd never seen before.

"Mr. Grayson Crandall?"

"Yes." The man handed him some papers and left. Gray frowned, opening them.

"What the hell?" he sputtered, reading the contents. This had to be a mistake. A big mistake. And Bob had a lot of explaining to do.

Within minutes, he was in his truck and headed for Sealy, Texas. When he turned into B & B Thoroughbred Farms, Gray saw a black BMW in front of him. Mariel. Evidently she wanted answers, too. It had been a long time since he'd seen her and he was afraid seeing her now would spark his temper. But this was about Chloe, not her mother. He and Mariel would have to get along because there was no way in hell he was losing his daughter.

MARIEL SAW THE WHITE truck as it parked beside her. Gray. She hadn't seen him since Chloe had opened her gifts last

Christmas morning, and she didn't want to see him now. It was too painful. But she got out of the car and met him at the front of his truck, pulling her coat tightly around her against the chilly December breeze. He usually wore a Stetson, but today his head was bare. The wind tousled his brown hair and she noticed the gray at his temples. At forty-two, age looked good on him. Well over six feet, he walked with an easy, confident swagger, except today he hurried toward her and his dark eyes were angry—just like they'd been so many times in the past four years when they'd seen each other.

"What's going on with Chloe?" he demanded, clutching the divorce papers in his hand.

"I don't know. That's why I'm here." She answered as calmly as she could.

"How was she on her birthday?"

He was good at firing off questions—one of his annoying habits. She would have appreciated a cordial greeting to start this conversation. But as hard as she tried she couldn't stop the flush of guilt that warmed her cheeks.

His eyes narrowed. "You did see her." It was a statement, not a question.

She swallowed hard, the guilt about to choke her. "I had a high-profile murder trial I couldn't get away from."

"Not even for a couple of hours." At his sarcastic words, her defenses kicked in like a stubborn mule. Gray wasn't doing this to her.

"Why didn't *you* see her on her birthday?" she countered.

"I was guarding a federal judge and I explained that to Chloe."

"Well, I explained my situation to her, too."

He looked into her eyes and her heart flip-flopped. She hated that he could still do that to her—make her feel young, vulnerable and so very foolish.

"You're very calm about this," he remarked.

"And you're very angry, which isn't going to accomplish anything."

"It would help to show some emotion, Mariel. Our daughter is trying to divorce us." He held up the legal papers.

She pressed her lips together. "I'm well aware of that. I plan to talk to Bob, then go see my daughter." She headed up the walk to the front door.

"Our daughter." He hurried after her. "Sometimes you seem to forget that."

"I never forget that," she replied, ringing the bell.

"What do you mean?"

She turned to him. "I'm not arguing with you. It's always been a waste of my time."

"Since when do you argue?" he retorted. "You shut down, shutting me and everything else out."

"How can you—"

The door suddenly opened and Bob stood there, puffing on a pipe. "Thought I heard voices. Come in. I've been expecting you."

They followed him into his study. "What the hell are you trying to pull?" Gray slammed the divorce papers on the desk.

Bob sat down and laid his pipe in an ashtray. That sweet, pungent smell drifted to Mariel and a familiar suffocating feeling came over her. Her father had smoked a pipe, and Mariel remembered all the times her mother complained about it and told him about the harmful side effects of the tobacco. She would always associate that smell with him. She could almost hear her mother's voice.

"I've been retained by Chloe to represent her in the divorce proceedings." Bob's words brought her back to the present.

"She's a kid, Bob," Gray reminded him. "And you have no

case." He tapped the papers. "Abandonment. Neglect. That's crap and you know it."

"Do I?" Bob leaned back in his chair. "I get a different story from Chloe."

"What has she told you?"

"Have a seat." Bob waved a hand toward some high-backed leather chairs.

They both complied.

"When was the last time you spoke to Chloe?" Bob asked.

"I talked to her the day after her birthday and she seemed upset then." Mariel set her purse on the floor and crossed her legs. "I've called every day since, but I always miss her. She hasn't returned any of my calls."

"Same here," Gray added. "Now I know why."

"You haven't talked to your twelve-year-old daughter in days," Bob went on. "Hasn't that bothered either of you?"

"Of course it has," Mariel snapped. "But Elaine assured me Chloe was fine." She took a breath. "There's no case here, Bob, so why are you doing this?"

The colonel leaned forward. "I was there for Chloe's birthday party. Elaine had invited several of the neighbors, but spending her birthday with a group of old codgers isn't very appealing to a young girl. And I can't blame her. She kept staring out the window, looking down the road waiting for one of her parents to show up. Guess what? Neither showed and neither called while I was there. I could see how that upset Chloe. When she came up with the idea to divorce you—and let me say right here that it was totally her idea—I agreed to help her. Because personally I think you two need to take a good look at what you're doing to your daughter."

Mariel stared down at her clasped hands.

Gray shifted uneasily in his chair. "Did Chloe say anything else?"

"Yes. She feels like a burden to you and if you didn't have to worry about penciling her into your busy schedules, you might be happy again. She's under the impression she's the reason you're not. I think Chloe would like some peace in her family life. She feels at home here on the ranch with Elaine and that's where she wants to stay."

"Is Elaine supporting this?" Mariel asked with a hint of surprise.

"I doubt if Chloe's told Elaine anything. As I told you, this is Chloe's idea."

Mariel reached into her purse for her checkbook. "How much does Chloe owe you? I'll pay for your work so far, but you and I both know this petition is bogus."

"The financial part is between Chloe and me. If I were you, I wouldn't be so quick to pull out the checkbook. Chloe doesn't need your money. She needs your love and your time."

At that, Mariel walked out without another word.

Gray stood and jammed both hands through his hair. "I want to smack you, Bob, and I'm not sure why. Maybe for exposing my failure and my weakness."

"I'm not doing this to hurt you or Mariel. You're good parents, but you've gotten a little side-tracked." Bob reached for his cap and settled it on his head. "I wish I'd had someone to point that out to me when my wife and I divorced. My son was ten and my wife took him to Philadelphia to live with her parents. After that, I saw my son very little and I did nothing to change that. Now I'm lucky if I see him twice a year—that is, if I make the effort to go to Philadelphia. He never comes here and that hurts." Bob got to his feet. "Don't make the mistake I did. Don't let pride or your job stand in the way of seeing your daughter. Chloe's a wonderful young girl and you're missing a lot. Take that piece of advice from an expert."

Gray swallowed and shook Bob's hand. "I assure you we'll get this straightened out."

"Go easy on Chloe. She's a very sensitive girl."

Gray nodded and walked to his truck.

GRAY PARKED IN FRONT OF the old ranch house where he was raised—a two bedroom white frame house, shaded by oak trees, with a chain-link fence around it. Two barns stood out back and a hay field lay to his left. In the distance he could see cattle grazing on winter grass. He grew up wanting to get away from here, away from having crap on his boots, hay down his shirt collar and calluses on his hands. But every time he came back he felt a tranquility he couldn't explain. All he knew was that a part of him belonged here.

Life was simple and easygoing. Maybe that's what Chloe liked, or maybe she enjoyed having his mom around twenty-four hours a day. He and Mariel hadn't been there for Chloe, and that wasn't an easy thing to admit. He had to see his daughter.

Bursting through the front door, he saw Mariel already seated in the living room talking to his mother.

Elaine turned to her son. "Gray, is this true? Chloe hired Bob to *divorce* you?"

He stared at her. In worn jeans, a flannel shirt and boots—what she always wore on the ranch—his mother's petite frame seemed thinner and her brown hair was almost completely gray. He hadn't noticed that before. His mother was getting older.

He kissed her cheek. "Yes. It's true."

"Chloe's been upset since her birthday. She's been nervous

lately, running out of the house when the phone rings, or going to hide in the bathroom."

"She didn't want to talk to us." Gray knew this now.

"You didn't know anything about this?" Mariel asked.

"Of course not." Elaine bristled, at the question.

"She wants you to have custody," Mariel added.

"Well, that's what I have now, isn't it? You two are so busy you never have time for her. It's finally gotten to Chloe."

"Don't start, Mom."

"Oh, son, I haven't even begun. But I will tell you one thing, I'm on Chloe's side—one hundred per cent and then some."

"Yes. We know."

"Good. I hope you plan to spend some time with her and let her know you care about her."

"I plan to. I'm not sure about Mariel's schedule."

He received a frosty stare for his remark.

Gray looked around. "Where's Chloe?"

"She's outside. We just finished feeding the cattle and she's racing Flash. I'll go get her."

"No." Gray caught his mother's arm. "We're going to surprise her this time. Our vehicles are parked out front so she won't know we're here."

"Now, Gray."

"Don't worry, Mom. We'll handle Chloe with the utmost care."

"You better. I'll make a pot of coffee."

Mariel sat on the brown tweed sofa and Gray took a seat beside her. An unwelcome silence hung between them.

"How do you want to do this?" Gray finally asked. The scent of her perfume was doing a number on his senses.

"Let me talk to her first."

"Why?" He stared at his ex-wife. At forty, she looked as beautiful as when he'd first met her. There were subtle changes, like her taut expression and her blond hair pulled back into a knot at her nape. Gray didn't like her hair like that, and he wanted to take out the clip and run his fingers through the silky tresses like he had many times in the past. But those days were over.

"Because you'll get angry."

"You're acting as if I have an irrational temper."

She closed her eyes briefly. "Gray, please. Let me talk to Chloe."

The twinge of sadness in her voice made him give in. It was the first sign the divorce papers had hit her hard.

"Okay." He rubbed his hands together. "I want what's best for Chloe. Obviously, we've failed in that respect."

"Yes. We're both to blame."

Gray nodded. "I…"

His voice trailed away as Chloe burst into the room, running to Elaine.

"Gran, you should see. Flash is awesome. Luis was timing me, but he was doing it in Spanish and I got all mixed up. It was fast, though. Faster than ever." Chloe took a breath, staring at Elaine. "Gran, why are you looking like that? It's like you've seen a ghost or…"

Chloe turned her head and saw Mariel and Gray. The color drained from her face.

"Oh. You're here."

Chapter Three

"Hi, Chloe," Gray said.

Chloe ran her hands down the front of her jeans, a gesture Mariel knew meant her daughter was nervous. "I guess you got the divorce papers?"

"Yes, we did," Mariel answered, and patted the space beside her on the sofa. "Come sit. We need to talk."

Chloe plopped down in the overstuffed chair instead, a move that didn't escape Mariel. Usually when she and her daughter had been apart for any length of time there were lots of hugs and kisses. Today there was awkward silence.

As she grappled with this, she noticed her daughter's worn jeans, knit top and muddy boots. Her long blond hair stuck out in disarray around her face and her bangs hung in her eyes. Mariel had promised to take Chloe to get her hair cut. She'd forgotten and the guilt of that was almost unbearable.

"Before you say anything," Chloe began, "I'm not going back to that school in Houston. I hate it."

"Is that what this is about?" Mariel asked. "You don't like your school?"

"It's about—" Chloe kicked at the hardwood floor with her boot. "Why did you have me? You don't have time for me."

"We had you because we wanted a child. Your father and I both love you and we want to do what's best for you."

"The best thing for me is to stay here with Gran."

"You don't get to make those decisions," Mariel told her.

"Fine." Chloe jumped to her feet. "Colonel Bob said I had to abide by your decision, but I'm not going back to that school and you can't make me."

Chloe darted toward her room, but Mariel leaped over the coffee table and caught her before she could reach the door. "Sweetie." She smoothed Chloe's hair, desperately needing to touch her child. "I had a reason for putting you in that school."

"What?" Chloe mumbled, her head down. "I liked my other school. Why did you have to move me?"

Gray had come to stand beside them and Mariel stiffened. She had to tell Chloe the truth and Gray wasn't going to like it.

Mariel continued to touch Chloe, her hair, her face. If she didn't, she'd break into so many pieces. She drew a long breath. "I deal with hardened criminals every day. One of them...threatened my life and the FBI felt I needed to put you in a safe place."

"What!" Gray's voice was sharp and angry. "My daughter's life was in danger and you kept that from me?"

"Her life wasn't in danger." Mariel gritted her teeth. "I just wanted her in a secure private school where a close watch is kept on the students and on visitors to the school."

"I'm her father. I should have been notified of this."

"I tried, but you were out of town."

"I wasn't out of town forever," Gray shouted. "This is just like you, Mariel, to keep things from me."

"I did what I thought was best and—"

"Go ahead and argue." Chloe pulled away from Mariel. "That's all you do, anyway, and it's always over me. If you didn't have me, you wouldn't have a reason to argue. Go away and leave me with Gran." Chloe ran to her room and slammed the door.

GRAY SUCKED AIR INTO his lungs and tried to get his emotions under control. His child's life had been threatened and he hadn't known. For weeks he'd been guarding a pompous judge when he should have been guarding his daughter.

"I'll talk to her." Elaine moved toward Chloe's room.

"No, Mom. We'll handle it."

"You're not—"

"Mom, please."

"Okay. I'm going outside. Coffee's in the kitchen."

Elaine walked out and Gray turned to Mariel, who was sitting on the sofa with her face buried in her hands. At the sight, the anger in him subsided and he sat next to her.

"You should have told me."

"Yes. I should have." She wiped at her eyes. "I should have kept trying to reach you then, but I wanted Chloe somewhere safe immediately."

"You said you took her out of the other school because of all the violence."

"I was unhappy with the school for a long time, and the threat just precipitated things." She reached for her purse and pulled out a tissue.

"Did the FBI apprehend the guy?"

"Yes, and they determined he wasn't as dangerous as they'd thought. But I kept Chloe in the private school because I thought it was better for her. I also had the security system updated in the condo for my own peace of mind."

There was a tense pause. Warm, soothing sunlight filtered through the windows.

"How are you now?"

"Fine. I was a little scared at first, but I had a bodyguard."

It should have been me.

Mariel glanced in the direction of Chloe's bedroom. "How did we get to be such terrible parents?"

"By getting divorced."

"Let's not rehash that, Gray."

"At some point we're going to have to. But right now we've got to focus on our daughter."

"Then let's talk about her," Mariel suggested. "How do we deal with this?"

"I don't like the thought of Chloe being unhappy in school."

Mariel twisted her tissue. "We could make other arrangements for the New Year."

"She wants to stay in Sealy."

She glared at him. "I'm not giving Elaine custody of my daughter. Chloe's twelve. She doesn't know what she wants."

"She knows enough to hire an attorney."

"That's because she's familiar with Bob and…" Her words trailed off.

He kept his gaze on the trembling curve of her lip. "I'm glad that bothers you, because it sure as hell bothers me."

"Yes," Mariel admitted. "I'm just not sure what to do about it and our arguing doesn't help."

Neither said anything for several minutes.

"Do you have any vacation time left?" Gray finally asked.

"I was planning to take some time at Christmas to spend with Chloe."

Gray used to look forward to the holidays—their Christmases filled with love and excitement. Now they were tense and stressful. Ever since the divorce, Chloe spent Christmas

Eve with Mariel, then Gray would stop by early the next morning to watch Chloe open her gifts. Afterward, he and Chloe went to his mother's to spend Christmas day.

Chloe's birthday was so close to the holidays that last year they had celebrated it at Christmas, thinking that it didn't matter to Chloe. This year, since he couldn't get away for her actual birthday, he planned to do the same thing. He realized now how much making both days special mattered to Chloe. Neither he nor Mariel wanted to explain to her that her parents didn't want to be in the same room for any length of time. Well, it was time to put their preferences aside for their daughter's sake.

"Can you take enough time for a real vacation?"

"I haven't had a vacation since—" Mariel was thoughtful for a minute "—we took Chloe and her friend, Jennifer, to Disney World."

"That's about the last one I had, too." Gray remembered it well. They'd been talking about having another child before Chloe got any older. Every stolen chance was spent trying to make it happen. Then disaster struck. A week after they'd returned home, Mariel's parents died in a plane crash. Instead of having a child, Mariel and Gray got a divorce and their lives were never the same. He couldn't dwell on the past now, though.

"That was right before the crash," he said, watching her face.

"Please." She touched her temple. "I don't want to talk about that."

After the accident, Mariel hadn't cried—she'd gone numb. The shattered look in her eyes haunted him and nothing he did or said could take away or ease her pain. She just wanted to be left alone and wouldn't even let him touch her. In the end, she'd asked him to move out saying she needed some time alone. He talked until he was blue in the face, trying to get her to open up or at least change her mind. Two months later she told him it would be best if they divorced. Gray was stunned. He still didn't understand how their marriage had fallen apart.

"You're going to have to talk about it someday," he couldn't help but say.

"Right now my concern is Chloe and this situation."

"Well, it's eight days until Christmas and I suggest we spend it here on the ranch with Chloe—all of us together. After Christmas we can decide what to do to make sure Chloe grows up happy and healthy."

"There's not enough room here for all of us."

"We've done it before."

"We were married then and shared a bed while Chloe slept with Elaine."

"We'll figure out something, Mariel. Everything doesn't have to be perfect."

"I suppose." She fiddled with the tissue. "And it will give us the time we need to make the right decision."

"Exactly." He glanced at the tall, freshly felled cedar standing in front of the living room window. "Mom already has the tree up."

Mariel followed his gaze. "But it's not decorated. I guess Chloe wanted to wait until we were here. Remember when she was about two and you had to hold her up so she could place each ornament on the tree? You or I couldn't do it. She had to personally do it herself."

"Yes. She's very bossy about the Christmas tree." He looked at her. "So what do you say? Want to spend a week on the ranch?"

"Yes. I think we need to." She heaved a heavy sigh and his eyes strayed to the rise and fall of her breasts. His fingers ached to touch, to rekindle…

They stared at each other, both lost in memories—memories of the good times. Gray was the first to look away. "I'll get Chloe."

Before he could move, Chloe's door opened and she came out, her eyes red, her hair hanging in her face.

Gray held out his arms. "Come here, baby girl."

Chloe flew across the room into her father's arms. "I didn't mean it when I said for you to go away," she cried into his chest.

Gray held her tight. "I know, baby, and I'm sorry I missed your birthday. But I do love you. Your mother loves you and we're both so sorry we've neglected you lately. We have never abandoned you, though."

Chloe eased herself down to sit between her parents, chewing on her hair. "Sometimes it feels like it."

It was strange to Mariel that Gray was being the affectionate parent, the one to break the ice. She used to be the loving, animated one, giving hugs and kisses for no reason other than she was happy. Why was she so different? Her emotions were frozen, and no matter how hard she tried she couldn't break free. She'd hurt her daughter, and she hadn't been able to save her marriage. Now she would have to find a way to live again—for Chloe.

And for Gray, too.

Mariel scooted closer, gently taking Chloe's hair out of her mouth. "Your father and I have been talking and we've decided, if it's okay with Elaine, to spend the days before Christmas here on the ranch."

Chloe's eyes lit up. "Really?"

"Yes. Then we'll make a decision about your school and your future. Just trust us to make the right one for you."

"Okay." Chloe went into Mariel's arms, and Mariel kissed her face, her hair. "Thank you, Mama."

"We've been absent a lot lately and your father and I are going to change that."

"Cool." Chloe smiled, then it quickly faded. "I just don't want to be a burden to you."

"Oh, baby." Mariel's hand trembled across Chloe's hair. "You're not. Your father and I have very busy jobs, but you're always on our minds."

Gray pinched her cheek. "Always."

"But if you let me stay here with Gran, you wouldn't have to worry about me. Gran needs my help, too. She can barely pick up a bale of hay, and with my help it's so much easier. I can drive the truck and tractor to help with feeding the cows and horses. I like it here. Please let me stay."

Gray saw that shattered look in Mariel's eyes and quickly intervened. "We'll talk about it after Christmas. Right now your mother and I have to go back to the city to get some clothes. But first I have to talk to Mom."

Almost on cue, Elaine came through the back door. She looked at the three of them. "Good. Smiles—that's what I like to see."

Gray got to his feet. "Mom, would it be okay if Mariel and I stayed here until Christmas?"

"Don't see why not. Chloe can sleep with me and Mariel can have Chloe's three-quarter bed. You, my son, will get the sofa bed."

Gray frowned. "Yeah. I remember the lumpy thing. Tell me you've gotten a new one."

"'Fraid not."

Mariel found herself smiling at Gray's expression and it felt good. "I can take the sofa bed," she offered.

"No. No." Gray shook his head. "That bed and I are good friends."

"I'm younger. I can sleep on the sofa bed," Chloe piped up.

"Poor old Dad is not so old that he can't sleep on a lumpy bed."

Chloe giggled, then said, "We have to have rules."

"Rules?" Gray's frown deepened.

"Yes." Chloe held up one finger. "Rule number one—no arguing."

Gray and Mariel looked at each other. "Deal," they said in unison.

Two fingers went up. "No cell phones. You can return calls once a day."

"What do you think?" Gray asked Mariel.

"I can manage," she responded.

"Deal," Gray said.

"And we have to make plans for Christmas," Chloe told them.

"What kind of plans?" Gray asked.

"We have to make all the decorations for the tree. We can't make the lights, of course, but everything else we make."

Gray hesitated. "Where do you come up with these ideas?"

Chloe shrugged. "They just pop into my head."

"We need to do something about that," Gray said to Mariel.

Mariel suppressed a grin. "I think it's too late."

"Chloe—"

"Without any arguing or complaining," Chloe added for good measure.

Gray pretended to think for a minute. "Oh. Okay."

"Thanks, Daddy, Mama." Chloe threw her arms around them. "This is going to be the best Christmas."

"No more talk about divorcing your parents." Gray kissed her cheek.

"No more talk about divorce," Chloe echoed, beaming from ear to ear.

Elaine went to finish up the chores, but she took the birth-day cake out of the freezer and they had another party with just the three of them, laughing, singing and teasing. Soon Gray and Mariel left to make arrangements for the time they'd be spending on the ranch.

Chloe hurried to her room, opened a drawer and pulled out her journal. Buffy lay on her bed asleep.

"You sleep too much," she said to the cat. "You missed Mama and Daddy."

She laid the journal on the bed and, kneeling on the floor, flipped through it to find her last entry. Page after page one word stood out—*waiting*. She found her place and began to write.

The arrival: My parents arrived today and it wasn't bad at all. At first I almost lost my dinner, but later we were able to talk. They still love me. I guess that's what I needed to hear. And we're spending Christmas together. That's to-tally cool. Now I have eight days to make them fall in love again. If they love me, they have to love each other. Colonel Bob said to expect the unexpected. I'm expect-ing a miracle.

Chapter Four

GRAY AND MARIEL WORKED out their schedules and settled in for Christmas on the ranch. Their goal now was to spend time with their daughter.

Leaning on the fence, Gray and Mariel watched Chloe race Flash around the oak trees to the pond and back. The air was brisk and invigorating and dark clouds hovered overhead with the threat of rain.

"She *mucho* good," Luis commented, loading bags of range cubes into the bed of an old truck.

"Yeah, she's getting better all the time." Gray turned to help him.

"Good you're home, Mr. Gray," Luis said. "I need to go to Mexico for Christmas, but Mrs. Crandall don't do so good by herself. Her right knee's been bothering her and she's slowing down."

Gray had noticed that his mother wasn't feeling all that well. "Don't worry, Luis. You go home and I'll take care of my family."

"*Gracias,* Mr. Gray." Luis nodded his head. "I go in the morning."

Chloe came running, out of breath. "Did you see me, Daddy?" Mariel was behind her.

"Yes. I saw. Flash is a mighty fast horse and you're—" he touched her flushed cheek "—an impressive rider."

Mariel put her arms around Chloe's neck from behind. "I've already told her that."

Gray looked into Mariel's bright eyes and for the first time in four years she seemed happy. But he saw the glimmer of pain that was always there. Why couldn't she talk to him? That's what hurt the most—her shutting him out.

"Time to feed the cows." Luis' words interrupted his thoughts.

"Why don't you put out the round bales of hay with the tractor and I'll handle the feed," Gray suggested. Bogey and Spence were on top of the sacks waiting for a ride.

"Gracias." Luis headed for the tractor as Elaine came into the barn.

"Why is everyone standing around?" she asked. "We need to get this feed to the cows. It'll be dark soon and it looks like rain."

Gray put an arm around her shoulder and again thought how thin she was getting. "We have it under control, Mom. Mariel, Chloe and I are feeding the cows and Luis is taking care of the hay. So you go to the house and relax."

"Relax?" Her brow held grooves of displeasure. "I don't know the meaning of the word. I'm not used to sitting around."

"Well, get used to it. While I'm here, you're off duty."

"Gray."

He gave her a nudge toward the door. "Go watch TV or read a book or just put your feet up."

"Okay." She took a couple of steps. "I can make supper."

"No. I'm taking everyone out to eat."

"This is ridiculous. What will I do?" But she headed for the house mumbling something under her breath he didn't quite catch.

Gray turned to Mariel and Chloe. "Okay, ladies. Who's driving and who's putting out feed?"

"I'm driving," Chloe answered immediately. "I can drive really good. Just watch."

"Chloe…" His voice faded away as she opened the door to the truck and jumped in.

He looked at Mariel. "That means you and I do all the work." He grabbed her hand. "Come on." They hopped onto the tailgate.

"Gray, I'm not sure about Chloe driving."

"We have to let her learn. She's twelve now."

"I know, but I still want her to be a little girl."

"Me, too."

They stared at each other, both realizing that when it came to Chloe, there were a lot of things they did agree upon.

"Ready?" Chloe shouted.

"Ready?" Gray whispered to Mariel, and she felt his breath on her cheek. She nodded, not trusting her voice.

"Ready," Gray shouted back.

The truck slowly began to move out of the barn and down the road to the pasture. Mariel held on to the side as the ride became bumpy. "Are the dogs okay?" The dogs stood on the sacks facing the front, looking for cattle.

"Sure. They do this every day."

The truck stopped at a fence.

"You have to open the gate, Daddy," Chloe shouted again.

Bogey and Spence barked, getting impatient.

"Dammit." Gray jumped off the tailgate. "I knew there was something I hated about this deal."

"I'll open the next one." Mariel tried not to laugh at him. When Chloe stopped again, she quickly ran to open the gate. Light rain splattered her head, but she only smiled, feeling an exhilaration she hadn't felt in a long time. Could it be the company?

"Hurry up," Gray called. "Or we're going to get wet."

The light sprinkles stopped as they reach the designated pasture. Chloe honked the horn and cattle began to run from the bushes and woods, swarming around the truck like hungry bees. Bogey and Spence leaped to the ground to keep the cows away from the feed until it could be distributed properly.

Mariel climbed on top of the feed sacks, not particularly liking this close-up view. The animals were big and they made a lot of noise, mooing and bellowing. Some even started to butt heads in anger, especially two red and white-faced bulls who seemed more interested in fighting than eating.

Gray ripped open a sack, and as Chloe guided the truck forward, Gray dumped the cubes in a trail on the dried grass. The dogs were expertly keeping the cows away from the front of the truck so Chloe could drive without hitting them.

"You're not helping up there," Gray yelled over the noise.

Mariel eased down from her perch, her heart in her throat. Grabbing a bag, she tried to open it and couldn't.

"Pull here," Gray instructed, showing her how to open the sack. The bag opened and she started to drop the small tube-shaped cubes on the ground as Gray was doing.

"Don't throw the bags out. The cows will eat them and it's harmful for their digestive system. We take the empty ones back to the barn and burn the lot."

"Okay." She continued to rip sacks and empty the sweet treat for the cattle, who were gobbling them up. Finally the last sack had been emptied onto the ground.

"To the barn, Chloe," Gray hollered.

The dogs jumped into the bed and the truck slowly chugged

its way homeward. Maricl sat on the sacks, as did Gray, to keep them from flying out.

It would be dark in a few minutes and a shadowy silhouette seemed to be closing around them. She rubbed her hands together to keep them warm. The temperature kept dropping but luckily the rain stayed away.

"It's very peaceful here," she said, listening to the sounds of the cattle and the hum of the truck. The trees in the woods were bare, but a few green cedars stood out among them. In places, leaves covered the ground in different shades of brown. It was definitely winter in Texas.

"Yeah. It's hard to believe that Houston's not far away— a completely different world."

"You told me many times that you couldn't wait to get away from here. Now I'm wondering why."

"I was young and stupid with a head full of dreams."

"You always wanted to be a lawman instead of a cowboy."

"Yep. But the cowboy in me surfaces now and then and I always come back to the ranch. Suppose I always will."

"Chloe's like that, too. She loves it here and I'm beginning to see why."

He buttoned his lined denim jacket. "Are you thinking of letting her stay here?"

"No. I'm just trying to see this from her point of view. After Christmas I'll arrange for her to attend her old school, if that's okay with you."

"I want her to be happy."

"Me, too," she said, her voice low. "And we have to be there for her. We can't keep letting Elaine raise our daughter. That's not acceptable to me anymore."

"I agree."

She looked at him. "We have to stop arguing about Chloe."

He stared back at her. "I don't want to argue about Chloe. But you know why I'm angry, yet you do nothing to change that."

At the tone of his voice, she locked her fingers together until they were numb. This claustrophobic feeling wasn't acceptable anymore, either. She had to conquer this, and the only way to do that was to share it. To finally tell Gray…

"I'll try. I really will."

Bogey lay down by Gray and he rubbed the dog's head. "Good. That's a start."

They rode in silence and Mariel gazed at the wintry landscape. She felt a connection with the simplicity of the land, felt a need to have her life back. "I was raised in the city and I don't know anything about ranch life. But at least I know how to ride because you taught me. Tomorrow I'm going riding with my daughter."

Chloe stopped at a gate. "Your turn or mine?" Gray asked.

Mariel sighed, then ran to open the gate and soon hopped back on the tailgate. "You really don't like to open gates, do you?"

"Every kid who grew up on a ranch has the same feeling. It's the first chore he's given and he's eager to pass it down to younger brothers and sisters, except I didn't have any so it stayed my job. I got really sick of it."

"Poor Gray." She tried to commiserate, but it came out as a tease.

"You just…"

The truck rolled into the barn and the conversation came to an end. The dogs jumped out and Mariel and Gray gathered up all the bags and took them to the trash barrel, then they hurried to the house with Chloe between them as the rain started again. Bogey and Spence raced ahead.

"How did I drive?" Chloe was eager to know.

"Wonderful." Mariel wrapped an arm around Chloe's waist.

"Like a pro," Gray added.

"I can get a learner's permit when I'm fifteen."

Gray groaned as he hung their coats on the pegs in the laundry room.

Chloe giggled, then asked, "Where're we going to eat, Daddy?"

"Anywhere you want, baby girl."

"Let's ask Gran." Chloe ran into the living room and came to a complete stop in the doorway.

Elaine slumped in her chair, her feet on a footstool. A fire burned warmly in the fireplace, the TV blared and a magazine and Buffy lay in her lap. But she was sound asleep.

Gray felt a stab of guilt. His mother was overworked and tired. He should have noticed this sooner. They tiptoed back into the kitchen.

"I don't think we should wake her," he said.

"I don't, either," Mariel agreed. "We'll just fix something here." She opened the refrigerator. "Elaine has hamburger meat thawed out. She was probably going to make a meat loaf, but that will take too long."

"I know what we can make." Chloe beamed, pulling out a frying pan. "We'll make Gran's easy soup. Gran and me make it all the time."

"What's in it?" Mariel asked.

"We'll brown the meat with salt and pepper and diced onion, then add two cans of ranch-style-bean-and-minestrone soup with a can of tomatoes. It's delicious."

Gray straddled a barstool and watched them, remembering how Chloe loved to work in the kitchen. Mariel looked happy, laughing with her daughter, and the pained expression was nowhere in sight. But he knew it would return. It always did.

ELAINE WOKE UP AND LOOKED around. "What time is it?"

"Time for supper," Gray told her. "So let's eat."

"What?" Elaine got to her feet. "I haven't even started anything."

"Don't worry, Elaine," Mariel said. "Chloe and I have it ready."

They ate supper with comfortable chatter as their accompaniment—mostly Chloe's. Gray wouldn't let Elaine help with the dishes and sent her back to the living room. She didn't protest too much and Gray knew she was grateful for the break.

Chloe went to feed the dogs, then took a bath while Gray and Mariel finished in the kitchen.

"I think we need to do all the work while we're here so Elaine can get some rest." Mariel folded the dishcloth and laid it over the sink.

"I was thinking the same thing." Gray leaned against the cabinet. "I never thought the ranch was getting to be too much for her. I hadn't even noticed. That doesn't make me feel very good. Before I know it my mom will be trying to divorce me, too."

"Your mother adores you and Chloe does, too. Her divorce was just a bid for attention and she was right. We have neglected her."

"Did I neglect you?" His eyes held hers, demanding a straight answer.

She looked away. "I'll check on Chloe."

He caught her arm. "You always do that, Mariel. Push me away. Shut me out. But we're going to talk about what happened in our marriage. If not now, then tomorrow or the next day because I'm not letting this drop. It's too important to me, to Chloe, to all of us. And you said you'd try."

She pulled away and went toward the bathroom, and Gray said a curse word under his breath.

Outside the bathroom door, Mariel took a moment. Sitting on the back of a pickup with the freedom of the outdoors, it was easy to make promises. But as always, Gray was pushing her, and the more he pressured her, the more she closed up. Even after four years, the pain hadn't changed. It was still too raw to share, even with Gray. She wished he'd understand, but for him to do that, she'd have to tell him what had happened. And she couldn't—not yet.

Chloe came out of the bathroom in red flannel pajamas and fuzzy slippers. "Time to make decorations for the tree," she announced, pulling a big box out of the closet.

Elaine got up. "Think I'll take my bath now. I got the tree, put the lights on and helped Chloe buy all the items for her decorations. Now you young folks can finish it."

"Aw, Gran, you're gonna miss all the fun." Chloe hugged her.

Elaine kissed her cheek. "Seeing you happy is all the fun I need." She gave her son and Mariel a knowing glance, then went into the bathroom.

Chloe dragged the box to the tree and Mariel sank down on the floor to help, trying to avoid looking at Gray. "What are we doing?" Mariel asked.

"I've got a plan," Chloe replied. "We're going to make a cowboy Christmas tree with faith, hope and love."

"No charity?" Gray took a seat on the sofa.

"Well, I haven't figured out what to make for charity yet." She pulled out a narrow rope from the box. "Tonight we'll make rope wreaths to hang all over the tree, tomorrow we'll tie red bandannas into bows." She held up a piece of barbed wire. "Then we'll make crosses out of this for faith, angels for hope and hearts for love."

"You do have a plan," Gray remarked.

"Yep. And we're going to do it as a family. Ring a bell with anyone?"

"Don't get smart," Gray said with a grin.

Chloe giggled and made a face at him.

"What's the plan for the wreaths?" Mariel asked.

Chloe settled down to business. "We cut the rope into ten-inch lengths, twist two pieces together like a braid and glue the ends together. Then tie a red bow with a sprig of holly around it. Simple."

"Okay," Gray said. "Now I have a plan. I'll cut the rope, Chloe twists and glues the ends and Mariel makes the bow."

"Great. I got the glue gun all hot and ready." They worked for more than an hour until all the wreaths were done, then Chloe hung them on the tree. "Tomorrow we'll work on something else and by Christmas Eve we'll have it finished."

Chloe gave them both kisses and ran off to bed with Elaine. Mariel put the box back in the closet while Gray unfolded the sofa bed. She watched him for a moment. His arms were strong, his movements sure, and yet he was the most gentle man she'd ever known. She missed him. She missed his touch. He wanted her to talk about her pain. Her inability to do so had destroyed her marriage, her life, her relationship with her daughter. Why couldn't she do something about it? Being around Gray made her want to and soon she'd have to make a choice. She hurried into the bathroom before he'd finished setting up the bed. There would be no more confrontations tonight.

CHLOE SLID OUT HER journal carefully, so as not to wake Gran, and wrote:

The tree! Tonight we worked on the tree as a family. Daddy isn't angry and Mama is talking more and she's even laughing. That has to be a good sign and Christmas is going to be great. I know it.

Chapter Five

The next morning, Mariel had coffee made and biscuits in the oven by the time everyone woke up. She didn't want Elaine to do any more work than necessary with two extra people in the house.

Gray trudged into the kitchen in his pajamas bottoms, his brown hair tousled from sleep. He never liked to wear the tops even in wintertime. Her lower abdomen warmed with familiar desire.

But all she said was "Please put on some clothes."

He rubbed the hair on his chest. "You've seen me like this a million times. Actually, I remember you liked me best this way."

"We're not married anymore and this is an entirely different situation."

He poured a cup of coffee. "You got that right."

"Let's don't argue."

"You got that right, too. I promised my daughter I wouldn't argue and I'm not, even though sometimes you make me mad as hell." With that, he went into the bathroom to get dressed.

The rest of the day went smoothly. After breakfast the four of them saddled up and went to check the herd. Bogey and Spence raced ahead, watching the cows as they arrived, waiting for orders. Gray asked about four older cows and Elaine said they hadn't had calves in more than a year and she'd been meaning to sell them. When Gray said they might as well do it now, Elaine agreed.

At the command from Elaine, the dogs went into action, heading the herd toward the corral attached to the barn. Mariel had never rounded up cattle before—it was definitely different than anything she'd ever done. When she'd first married Gray, she didn't know anything about horses, either, but they'd spent many weekends coming to the ranch, riding and enjoying the outdoors.

The cows clearly didn't like being coralled and several tried to escape, but Gray deftly brought them back with Bogey or Spence snapping at the escapees' feet. Gray was very good on a horse. But he was good at everything he did.

Clouds of dust swirled behind the cattle as they rushed into the large corral. Some began to fight one another, pushing and shoving, others raised their heads looking for a way out, bellowing and making snorting noises. Mariel feared the baby calves were going to get trampled.

Elaine and Mariel dismounted and tied their horses to the fence, climbing on top to get a better view. The dogs lay on the ground, watching intently. Gray went in on his horse, meandering through the cattle. Elaine pointed out which ones she wanted to sell and he cut them from the herd into another pen. Baby calves jostled around trying to find their mamas. Then Chloe opened the gate and the cattle rushed out, eager to escape.

Gray dismounted and looked at the four remaining cows. They were old and should have been sold long ago. It was a waste of money to keep feeding them. On a ranch, you continuously had to look at the bottom line. In her younger days, his mom would never have let this happen. He was going to have to find her more help.

"I'll load these up and take them to the auction," he told Elaine.

"I'm going, too, Daddy," Chloe called.

"I'm not staying behind." Mariel jumped off the fence.

While Gray hooked up the cattle trailer and backed it toward the loading chute, Mariel, Chloe and Elaine unsaddled the horses and fed them. Gray loaded the cattle and slammed the trailer gate shut. Then Mariel and Chloe climbed into the truck and they headed to the auction barn.

The place was a hive of activity, with trucks pulling trailers of cattle from nearby ranches lined up waiting to unload. Their time came and the cattle were tagged to be sold. The auction cowboys whooped and hollered, herding the cows into a pen.

Gray and Chloe went inside to give his mom's name and address. He saw a lot of familiar faces, people he recognized from his boyhood. He shook hands, enjoying that feeling of coming home. Most everyone knew Chloe by name. She was clearly liked in this small town and he felt like a proud papa, impressed with his daughter and her engaging personality.

Gray spoke with Ed Tarver, a nearby rancher and an old friend of his dad's, about an extra hand to work his mom's ranch. He said he'd do some checking, and Gray knew he could count on that. People kept their word around here. That was another good thing about being home—knowing people you could trust.

Back at the ranch, Mariel decided to take Chloe to get her hair cut and to do some shopping while Gray stayed behind to talk to his mother. He brought in wood and started a fire and Elaine busied herself making stew for supper. Wiping her hands on her apron, she came into the living room to relax for a moment.

"That feels good," Elaine said, holding her hands to the fire. "It'll probably get down in the forties tonight."

Gray eased on to the sofa. "We should have put central heat in this house long ago."

"The space heaters and fireplace keep the place warm."

"What's wrong with your knee?" He slipped the question in, hoping to catch her off guard.

"Nothing." Her brow creased. "Who told you it was bothering me?"

"Doesn't matter."

She sank into her chair. "It was Chloe, wasn't it?"

Gray shook his head. "What's wrong with your knee?"

"I slipped on the tractor and bumped it and it's been a little tender, that's all."

"Did you see a doctor?"

"Of course not. I bump myself all the time working this ranch."

"I'm going to hire some extra help. I spoke with Ed about it at the auction barn today." He expected an explosion, but all he got was quiet. It was so unlike his mother to not complain about people going out of their way to help her.

"I was actually thinking about leasing the pasture."

"What?"

She looked him straight in the eye. "I'm getting older, son, and I don't want to work until I die. I'd like to travel and see something of this world before that happens. The only place I've been out of Texas is Oklahoma, when you got married."

He was speechless. He never dreamed his mother wanted to do anything like that. She was a rancher, a homebody, and she never showed any interest in anything else. It occurred to him that maybe he hadn't been listening.

"I'd like to put on a pretty dress and go dancing. Your dad and I danced all the time."

"I'll take you dancing," he offered quickly.

"Don't be silly." She waved a hand. "You need to be dancing with Mariel."

"That's a little hard to do when she doesn't want to dance with me."

Elaine studied him. "You still love her. I know you do."

Gray stared at his hands. "My feelings have nothing to do with our problems."

"Staying away from Chloe, missing her birthday and expecting Chloe to understand is not the answer."

"I know, Mom."

"Then get your life straightened out."

"Yes, ma'am," he said like when he was a kid and had done something wrong. They burst out laughing, then they hugged.

Gray knew that after Christmas there would be a lot of changes in his life and with his family. He hoped he could live with them.

THE DAYS PASSED QUICKLY for Gray—too quickly. Mariel worked on the ranch and helped with the cooking and cleaning without one word of complaint. The impeccably dressed professional woman who never had a hair out of place now spent her days in jeans, boots and flannel shirts. Dirt from feeding cattle stained her clothes and her hair never stayed in its ponytail. Tendrils hung around her face and he thought she never looked more beautiful.

They went Christmas shopping together and every night they made more decorations for the tree. Mariel and Chloe tied red bandannas into bows. He cut the barbed wire into small pieces and Mariel and Chloe glued the parts together to make a cross. Chloe said it signified faith. To add to the Texan theme of the tree he had to cut old leather into the shape of a boot and glue it onto colored cardboard. After Chloe and Mariel added some detail to them, Chloe hung them on the tree. They cut hearts out of worn denim and glued them on a backing of red poster board, then they decorated them with glitter. Chloe wrote everyone's names on them. Even Colonel Bob and Luis got a heart. Chloe said the hearts were for love.

They found wild holly with red berries and mistletoe on the ranch and Chloe placed the sprigs all over the house. The angels were the last decorations they had to make, according to Chloe's plan. It was Christmas Eve and they had to be done tonight.

After supper Chloe took her bath, then pulled the box out of the closet. He and Mariel sank to the floor to help, and Elaine sat by the fire with Buffy on her lap.

"Tonight we have to make the angels cause it's Christmas Eve," Chloe announced.

"Where does she come up with this stuff?" Gray whispered to Mariel.

"I heard that," Chloe said, fishing fabric out of the box. She wagged a finger at her father. "No complaining."

"Yes, ma'am." He tried very hard not to laugh.

"The angels are for hope—hope for the future," Chloe explained. "We have to make the big angel to go on top first to bring the spirit of Christmas into our home. The angel has to be a cowboy because this is a ranch."

"And where did you learn all this?" Gray asked.

"I've been going with Gran to that little country church down the road and I've just added my own ideas."

"Which you have plenty of."

"Yes." Chloe made a face. "I take after Mama."

"Really?" Mariel glanced up from going through the box. "I didn't realize I was that creative."

"Sure you are," Chloe replied, looking at the tree. "See the pretty bows you made out of the bandannas. Daddy couldn't have done that."

"Wait a minute," Gray protested. "I cut the leather to make the boots and I cut the barbed wire for the crosses."

"That doesn't require much creativity, just a strong, steady hand."

"Okay. I'll take that."

"How do you want us to make the angels?" Mariel asked.

"Remember when I was in second grade and my class made angels for Christmas?"

"Yes."

"That's the way we're going to make them, only better."

"We made those out of small paper plates and doilies," Mariel said.

Gray remembered. After Chloe got home from school, they had to make angels to put on their own tree. They'd sat on the floor, like they were doing now, as a family, with Chloe giving instructions about how they had to be made. He was beginning to think that Chloe had more plans in her head than just the one for the Christmas tree.

"Yeah." Chloe held up white paper plates. "These are large 'cause the cowboy has to be big. We make a cut in the paper plates from the edge to the center." She cut a slit with the scissors. "Then overlap the edges to make cones and secure the edges with staples or glue. We have to make two—one for the top of the angel and one for the bottom."

With that done, Chloe reached for a small white piece of fabric and placed a small plastic ball in the center. Using a glue gun, Chloe attached the fabric around the ball and trimmed off the excess material to make the angel's head. "Now we fold a large doily in half and fit it over the cone, sticking a hat pin up through the cone and doily to secure the head. Add a little glue, Mama."

Mariel did as instructed.

"See? Simple," she said. "Are you paying attention, Daddy?"

"You bet."

"Good, 'cause we have to make several. And, Mama, you get to draw the face with flesh paint 'cause you're good at that, too."

Chloe found the paints and Mariel drew a face with eyes, nose and mouth. While it dried they made several more cones. Chloe made wings by pulling the back and front of the doily down over the cone and glued it, then folded the ends of the doily up so that two wings spread out at the sides.

"Since this is a cowboy angel, we have to make the bottom skirt out of denim. Gran and I cut out the fabric one night while watching TV." She picked up a round piece of denim. "We used the paper plate for a pattern to make it round. Daddy, you cut a strip of leather into a fringe and I'll glue it on." Gray hurriedly did the leather. Then Mariel helped her glue the top of the denim to the cone. The bottom they left full and flowing.

That done, they glued the angel top to the bottom skirt and gave it a moment to dry.

"Look what Gran and I found in the hobby store." Chloe held up a small western hat. "Isn't it cute?"

"Absolutely," Gray said, tongue in cheek. "Cutest hat I've ever seen."

"Be nice, Daddy."

"Yes, Daddy, be nice." Mariel smiled at him and he could feel the family rapport again—just like years ago.

"We have to make a halo." Chloe cut and curled a gold pipe cleaner and glued it to the hat, then she glued the hat to the head of the angel. "What do you think?" She held it up.

"Maybe a piece of red bandanna around the neck," Mariel suggested. "And some glitter on the wings and the skirt."

"Yes." They quickly added the changes and Chloe set it aside to let it dry.

Buffy sneaked over to investigate the angel. "It's not food, Buffy," Chloe said. "You can't eat it." Buffy crept to Elaine and jumped into her lap.

"Very nice," Elaine said, looking at the angel.

Mariel held her hands together. "It's beautiful."

"How many of these angels do we have to make?" Gray wondered if they'd be up all night.

"We have to make one for all our loved ones in heaven," Chloe told him. "Grandpa Crandall, Grandpa Todd and Grandma Todd."

The room became very quiet and Gray saw the look on Mariel's face—that pained, helpless expression. He wanted to stop Chloe, but also knew Mariel couldn't keep suppressing her feelings. She had to deal with her parents' deaths—one way or another.

"We cut Grandpa Crandall's top out of an old chambray shirt. Gran said he'd turn over in his grave if we made him out of a doily." Chloe kept talking, not noticing her mother's distress.

"That would be perfect for him," Gray said. "He was always a cowboy and he would have loved you, Chloe."

"Do you think so?"

"Definitely," Elaine agreed. "He would have spoiled you rotten."

"Oops." Gray laughed. "Too late. She's already rotten."

"I am not." Chloe made a face again.

Gray was hoping the bantering would bring Mariel into the conversation, but she never said a word, just kept concentrating on the angel in her hands. He wanted to grab her face, make her look at him, make her talk. But he'd tried that and it hadn't worked. Nothing worked.

"I got a hat for him, too. We can't put a lot of glitter on his angel cause Gran said he wasn't a glitter person, either."

"No, he wasn't." His father was a simple man with honesty and integrity ingrained in him. Being a cowboy didn't keep him from supporting Gray in his life's choices. He never pressured him to stay on the ranch. His father died the year Gray became a U.S. Marshal and Gray still missed him.

He helped Chloe make wings out of the chambray and Mariel glued the denim for the bottom, but she didn't speak. They worked in silence.

"That one is finished," Chloe said, laying it by the other. "Grandma Todd is next and she's definitely satin, isn't she, Mama?"

Mariel swallowed. "Yes."

"And lots of glitter 'cause Grandma liked nice things. Look." Chloe help up a tiny string of white beads. "I made a string of pearls for Grandma. She never went anywhere without her pearls—you told me that once. I bet she's wearing them in heaven, don't you think so, Mama?"

Head bent, Mariel didn't answer. She just kept helping Chloe put the angel together and Chloe didn't seem to need an answer. Gray felt as if he was watching an accident about to happen and he could do nothing to stop it.

Chloe laid the angel with the others. "Now for Grandpa Todd. I got him some starchy white material and black ribbon for a bow tie. It was kind of hard to come up with something for him, but Grandpa was tough, even though he didn't mean to be. That was just him. One time he told me I had to be a lawyer and I told him I was just a kid and I didn't know what I wanted to be. He said to succeed in life I had to make up my mind early. Grandma told me not to pay any attention to him. I gave him a hug and told him that I loved him and…"

Mariel jumped up and ran into the bathroom.

"Daddy?" Chloe looked at him with frightened eyes.

"It's all right, baby." Gray hugged her. "Your mom is still dealing with a lot of grief over her parents. I'll talk to her."

Elaine got up. "I'll make some hot chocolate."

Gray stood outside the bathroom door, wondering how to handle this. Wondering how to get his family back. And most of all, how to get his wife back.

Chapter Six

Gray opened the door and spotted Mariel sitting on the edge of the bathtub, crying with her face in her hands. When she saw him, she stood and wiped away tears.

"Are you okay?" he asked, stepping in and closing the door.

"Yes, yes. I'm fine." She tried to walk past him, but he caught her arm.

"You're not fine. You're falling apart because our daughter mentioned your parents. Chloe's worried that she's upset you."

"Gray, please." She attempted to pull away, but he drew her closer.

"What's bothering you? For God's sake, tell me what's bothering you."

"Gray..."

"It's been four years, Mariel. That's long enough and—"

She suddenly laid her forehead on his chest and he was stunned for a second. She usually avoided all contact with him.

"Mariel." He stroked her hair, her obvious pain almost more than he could bear. "Talk to me."

A sob caught in her throat. "Not now. I have to reassure Chloe."

She moved away and he let her. It was a step—a very big

step. From her response, he assumed they'd be talking later. He'd make sure they did.

They walked back into the living room and Chloe ran to her mother and hugged her. "I'm sorry, Mama. I didn't mean to upset you."

"It's okay, baby." Mariel soothed her. "I'm just a little emotional about my parents. Let's finish the angels."

"We don't have to," Chloe said.

"Sure we do," Mariel said, sinking to the floor. "We have to make angels of all our loved ones and put them on the tree. Isn't that the plan?"

"Yes." Chloe knelt down beside her and Gray followed suit. Together, they finished the angels in silence until Chloe stood. "Now we have to put them on the tree. Daddy, you have to put the one on top 'cause I can't reach it."

"Why not?" Gray asked, getting to his feet and grabbing Chloe around the waist and lifting her into the air.

Chloe giggled. "Daddy. I don't have the angel."

"Here it is." Mariel handed it to her.

Chloe giggled so much that she was having difficulty anchoring the angel.

"Hurry up, baby girl," Gray shouted, taking a labored breath. "I'm not Hercules."

Chloe giggled that much more, her fingers fumbling to secure the angel on top of the tree. "Done," she shouted, and Gray lowered her to the floor. Then she quickly positioned the other angels just as she wanted them and stood back to admire her handiwork.

Gray dropped onto the sofa and watched the glow on her face. Mariel sat beside him and they shared a secret glance. Their daughter was happy.

"The tree is beautiful," Elaine said, bringing hot chocolate and setting the cups on the coffee table. "A Texas down-home cowboy Christmas with angels."

"That's the theme. We're having a Merry Texmas," Chloe told them.

"A Merry Texmas?" Gray lifted an eyebrow.

"Yep. Just like Gran said, except I shortened it." Chloe picked up the mug with the most marshmallows. "This one's mine."

"As if we didn't know," Gray quipped, handing a mug to Mariel. He raised his cup. "Here's to a Merry Texmas." He smiled at Mariel and she smiled back. That was good. She hadn't completely shut him out.

Chloe squeezed between them, sipping on her chocolate. "Now we have to sing Christmas carols like we always do."

"Another part of the plan?" Gray winked at Chloe.

"Yep."

They sang several songs and finished with "Silent Night."

"That was lovely," Elaine said. "Now we have to put all the presents under the tree to make it complete."

For the next few minutes they retrieved presents from secret hiding places all over the house. They stood for a moment in front of the tree, just enjoying the moment.

Elaine yawned. "'Night, everyone. I'm going to bed. I have to be up early to put the chicken on for dressing."

Chloe kissed her. "Good night, Gran. Remember the Christmas tree lights have to stay on all night 'cause it's Christmas Eve."

"Yes, sweetpea. I'm very aware of your traditions."

Gray hugged his mom, as did Mariel. Then Mariel and Chloe washed the cups and put them away.

"Mama, I'll sleep with you tonight 'cause I don't want you to be sad. We can fit in the three-quarter bed."

"Thank you, baby. I'd like that."

Gray groaned inwardly. Of all nights for Chloe to suggest that. He had to find a way to get Mariel alone.

Mariel and Chloe went to bed and Gray took a shower. As he pulled out the sofa bed, he could hear them laughing and talking, and it seemed as if Mariel was okay. But she really wasn't and he knew that.

He lay down, cursing the bed. It was the lumpiest thing he'd ever slept on, and to make matters worse he had to sleep with the damn Christmas lights on. "Merry Christmas, Gray," he said to himself, tossing and turning. Then he relaxed and grinned. "Merry Texmas," he corrected himself. And he prayed this Christmas turned out as special as his daughter.

IN THE COZY BED, CHLOE chattered about Christmas, but Mariel only half listened. Her thoughts were on her reaction to Chloe talking about Mariel's parents. Gray was right. It was time to talk. She'd kept a secret to herself for so many years and it was crippling her, killing her. She couldn't keep it inside any longer.

Chloe fell asleep and Mariel crawled out of bed, careful not to wake her. She stroked Buffy and walked into the living room where the tree lights glimmered and a fire still glowed in the fireplace. Gray lay on his side, his back to her. How did she tell him what she needed to? What she had to?

The tree drew her near and she sat cross-legged in front of it, looking up at the angels. So many guilty feelings surfaced and tears streamed down her face. "I'm sorry," she whispered to the angels.

"Mariel."

She jumped as Gray dropped down by her.

"I'm sorry. I didn't mean to wake you."

"Sleeping on that nightmare is hit and miss." He glanced at the tree. "What are you doing?"

"Somehow I feel their presence here."

"Your parents?"

"Yes. Chloe's love brought them here."

"What about your love?"

"I don't think…" She couldn't put into words what she was feeling.

"Surely you don't doubt that they loved you?"

"No. I doubt whether I deserved their love."

"What are you talking about? Douglas and Lois adored you. You were their only child."

She linked her fingers together. She had to do it now. The fragrant scent of cedar drifted to her nostrils. In the semi-darkness the fire crackled and the old grandfather clock ticked in the background.

"You don't know the whole story." He didn't pressure her or demand that she tell him what she was thinking like he usually did. He just waited and that's what she needed—his patience, his understanding.

"Remember how we were trying to have another child?"

"Of course."

"I wasn't getting any younger and I wanted to do it before Chloe got much older. It was wonderful that year on vacation, sneaking away to be together. I was so excited. I just knew it was happening. My cycle was right. Everything was right."

"It was a happy time," he said quietly. "We were home a week when we got the call about the plane crash."

"My life stopped that day."

Gray didn't push, and she was able to go on. "My parents called that morning to say they were flying to Washington. I told Mom I was hoping to be pregnant when they returned. She was happy for us, but Dad wasn't. He took the phone from her and asked what was I thinking. He said if I wanted another child I should have had one after Chloe. Now it was too late. I had my career to think about and I needed to get my head on straight."

Her voice stalled. "I got so angry and I told him I resented that he tried to control my life and…and…I said I hated him. Those were the last words I said to him. He died before I could apologize. I…I…"

Gray slipped his arms around her and pulled her close. "Mariel, you had nothing to apologize for. He had no right to say that to you. It was our decision, not his."

She rubbed her face against his bare chest. "Mom called back and said he didn't mean a word he was saying, and when they got back from Washington they were coming to Houston so he could apologize in person. Those were her words, not his."

"You know your father and his hot temper."

"Yes. When Chloe was talking about him tonight, I realized how immature I was. I should have said, like Chloe, that I loved him, but it was my life and I hoped that he'd support me in our decision. After the crash, I couldn't get beyond all the guilt I felt."

"Is that why you couldn't talk to me?"

"Partly." His breath fanned her cheek and she leaned toward him. He kissed her neck, the side of her face. She breathed in his scent for a moment and pulled away.

"Mariel," he said. "Why do you hate for me to touch you?"

"I don't." She tucked hair behind her ears. "Every time I see you I want you to hold me, touch me and kiss me until all I can think about is you."

His eyes narrowed. "I've never gotten that impression."

"I made sure that you didn't."

His face darkened in the fire's glow. "Why would you do that?"

She glanced at the tree, studying the angels, and dredged up every ounce of courage she had. "There should be another angel on the tree."

He blinked. "What? Who?"

She looked at him. "Promise me you won't get angry."

"I won't get angry."

"Three weeks after my parents' deaths we had a big argument because you wanted me to talk and I wouldn't. I couldn't—not even to you. I left the house saying I had to be alone."

"Yes. You didn't come home until morning and I was worried sick."

"As I was driving away, I started cramping severely and I thought it was nerves, but I soon realized it wasn't. I drove to the emergency room and…and…miscarried our child. I didn't even know I was pregnant."

"What!" The room became so quiet that the tick of the clock sounded like a gun going off at intervals.

She dragged in a breath. "The doctor said the miscarriage was brought on by the stress and trauma of my parents' deaths. I lost our child. I killed it."

"Oh, my God, Mariel." He wrapped her in his arms and the warmth of him eased the tremors in her. "Why couldn't you tell me this?"

"I just couldn't," she said, and sobbed into his neck. "I felt as if I was being punished. I needed to be punished."

"Oh, Mariel." He rocked her back and forth.

After a while, her sobs subsided. "When Chloe was talking about the angels tonight, I so desperately wanted to say that there was another Crandall angel in heaven. I wanted to tell you, knew that I had to. I've been grieving too long." She hiccuped. "Chloe's right. I believe the spirit of Christmas has come into this room."

Gray reached for the box on the floor.

"What are you doing?" She wiped away tears.

"We're making an angel for Baby Crandall."

"Oh, Gray. That's a wonderful idea."

"But I have no idea how to do this. I wasn't paying close attention to Chloe's instructions."

She smiled through her tears. "Don't worry. I'm supposed to be the creative one."

Together they sat by the light of the tree and put together a small angel of all-white satin. Gray stood and placed it on the tree between Douglas and Lois.

Mariel looked into his eyes. "Thank you for being so understanding."

He gently touched her face, sending waves of comfort bolting through her—Gray's healing comfort. "I couldn't be anything else. You're hurting too much."

Looping her arms around his neck, she murmured, "Remember all the years we put out gifts for Chloe and ended up making love under the tree?"

"How could I forget? The tree has a completely different meaning for me."

A smile, a generous smile, tilted her lips. It was good to feel joy again. She softly touched his mouth. "Let's do that tonight."

He pulled her closer, pressing her curves into his and taking her mouth with mind-reeling intensity. Her stomach quivered with anticipation as they lay back on the floor. The warmth and crackle of the fire mingled with their sighs and moans. She ran her hands across his chest, his shoulders, loving the freedom of touching him again. "I've missed you," she whispered against his skin.

"Honey, I've missed you, too." He unbuttoned her pajamas

and she quickly slipped out of them. His fingers played their magic on her body. As his lips found her breasts, she moaned, her hands equally at work on him.

"Love me, Gray. All I want to feel is you."

His hardness pressed against her and she opened her legs, welcoming him, needing him with more urgency than she ever thought possible.

Neither of them thought about protection.

Neither wanted to.

Chapter Seven

When Gray woke up, his arms were empty and he felt the loneliness creeping back in. Had last night been a wonderful dream? It wouldn't be the first time he'd dreamed Mariel slept in his arms. Then he saw the angel they'd made on the tree and he relaxed. The smell of coffee filled the room and he knew Mariel was up making breakfast.

Their daughter, the hurricane, would be awake any minute. And even though she was past the age of believing in Santa Claus, she thoroughly enjoyed Christmas. Gray sat up, staring at the small angel. Mariel had been pregnant and he hadn't known—she hadn't, either. He guessed she'd dealt with the heartache and pain alone because that was the only way she could do it at the time.

Looking back, he could see how he'd pressured her to talk and he hadn't given her any time alone. He'd wanted to be there for her, but she'd needed that distance from him to deal with everything she was feeling, especially about her father and the loss of the baby. His persistence had pushed them further apart and her inability to talk had made the situation intolerable.

He'd needed to touch and hold her and she had needed just the opposite. Maybe he'd never understand how the female psyche worked. But this time he wasn't pressuring or pushing. He was going to be accepting and loving, and hopefully they could put their marriage back together. They hadn't talked about the future; they'd been too busy rediscovering each other.

Slipping out of bed, he headed for the kitchen. Mariel turned from the stove and smiled at him. She had on her pajamas, her hair in disarray around her face.

He took her in his arms and kissed her. "Good morning and Merry Christmas."

"Mmm." She deepened the kiss, pressing her body against his.

"I thought I dreamed last night," he murmured against her lips.

"No. It was real and wonderful." She rested her face in the crook of his neck. "I'm so sorry."

"We need to talk about the future." He kissed her hair.

"Mmm." Her tongue flickered inside his ear. "I do like you best this way." She gave him a quick kiss. "I'm getting distracted and our daughter will be bursting in here in a few minutes. Time to put wood on the fire. It's getting cool in here."

His hands trailed slowly down her back, cupping her behind. "I'm not. I'm very, very warm."

"Gray." A chuckle slipped from her throat.

Grinning, he went into the living room and slipped into his pajama top. He added wood to the fire and stoked it, then he straightened his bed and folded it up.

Elaine came out of her room. "Oh, my, I overslept."

"It's not even six, Mom, and it's Christmas morning. Merry Christmas."

"Same to you, son. I never sleep this late." She rushed into the kitchen.

"Merry Christmas, Elaine, and don't worry," Mariel said. "I have the chicken on for dressing and coffee's ready."

"Thank you, Mariel, and Merry Christmas to you, too."

"Damn, I forgot to get coffee," Gray said, headed for the coffeepot. "I really must be distracted."

"Or tired," Mariel whispered to him.

Before he could respond, Chloe's door opened and she charged in, shouting, "Merry Christmas! Merry Christmas! Merry Christmas!" She hugged and kissed everyone, then ran to the tree.

"I'll separate the gifts and then…" Her voice trailed away as she stared at the tree. "There's a tiny angel on the tree. Where did it come from?"

Gray looked at Mariel's face and he knew this would be the test. If she could talk about the baby to Chloe and his mother, she was on the road to recovery and there was hope for them—for the future.

He smiled at her and nodded, giving his support in silence.

Mariel put an arm around Chloe. "I've kept a secret for a very long time because when it happened, I couldn't deal with it. Last night when you were talking about the angels and hope for the future, I knew there was no hope until I told your father." She inhaled deeply. "When your grandparents died in that crash, I was pregnant. I didn't know until the trauma over their deaths caused me to lose the baby. I was still in grief and unable to handle another blow. I shut your father out, never telling him. I shut everyone out." Misty-eyed, she tucked hair behind Chloe's ear. "I told your father last night and we made the angel together."

"Oh, Mama." Chloe wrapped her arms around Mariel. "I'm sorry."

"I'm fine, baby." Mariel held her daughter. "You truly brought the spirit of Christmas into this house."

"Thank you." Chloe rested against Mariel. "Is that why you and Daddy separated?"

"Yes. It was my fault, not your father's."

"That's not true," Gray said. "It was my fault, too."

A look of love and understanding passed between them.

Chloe drew back. "I thought Daddy found another woman."

"What!" Gray was shocked. "Why would you think that?"

"Well, my friend Jennifer's parents got divorced 'cause her dad found a younger woman. I thought maybe you did, too."

Gray pinched her cheek. "Thank you very much for that confidence."

"I knew Mama didn't date and she was always so sad." Chloe shrugged. "So I figured it had to be you, Daddy, but I still loved you."

Gray grabbed her and tickled her until she giggled uncontrollably.

Elaine embraced Mariel. "I'm so sorry for all the pain you've been through."

"Thank you, Elaine."

"I lost a baby before Gray was born and John tried to console me, tried to comfort me with plans of having another child. I couldn't talk about it and I couldn't explain to him what I was feeling. It's intimate, private. We lose a part of ourselves and it takes a while to get that back, if ever. I'm so happy you're able to talk about it now."

Mariel squeezed her mother-in-law, knowing she understood in a way only a woman could. Talking was now the solace she needed.

"Presents. We have to open presents," Chloe shouted.

The next hour they spent laughing and opening gifts and there were no shadows or ghosts in the room, just angels and happiness. Mariel and Elaine fixed French toast for breakfast while Gray and Chloe picked up all the wrapping paper.

Elaine stayed behind to prepare Christmas dinner while the three of them went to check the herd.

Mariel never dreamed she'd love the outdoors this much. The brisk morning air and the peaceful scenery was breathtaking. She felt as if she'd been wearing dark glasses and they'd suddenly been removed and everything was brighter, clearer.

They checked the cattle and water troughs and everything was fine. Chloe raced toward them on Flash.

"I'm going to say Merry Christmas to Colonel Bob."

Before they could say a word, she and Flash were gone, flying over fences toward B & B Thoroughbred Farms.

Gray moved uneasily in the saddle. "Can you imagine what she's going to be like at eighteen or twenty? She's already opinionated, independent, and has more nerve than anyone her age should have."

"She's a lot like her grandpa Todd." Mariel had never noticed that before, but Chloe had a lot of her father's nerve and spirit, except Chloe had a soft heart. It was on the surface for the world to see, while Douglas Todd's was hidden deep inside. But as hard as he was at times, Mariel knew that he'd loved her. She hated that her last words to him had been so harsh but took comfort that he knew she loved him, too.

"Should I worry about that?" His eyes glittered.

"No. Chloe has us to guide her. With a little luck she won't try to divorce us again before she's eighteen."

Gray laughed and turned his horse toward the barn. "Race you back."

"You're on," she yelled as she kneed the horse and took off at a gallop, the dogs behind her.

As they neared the barn, Gray easily passed her. She jumped off and fell backward into a pile of hay, laughing and feeling young and alive again. Gray plopped down beside her, staring into her vibrant eyes. He caught her face and kissed her, bearing her further into the hay.

The kiss went on and neither wanted to stop. Finally Gray tore his mouth away. "Guess we should help Mom."

"Yes." Mariel sat up, brushing hay from her clothes. Gray helped her to her feet and they unsaddled the horses, then they walked to the house arm in arm. Bogey and Spence followed and settled into their spots by the back door.

A mouthwatering aroma greeted them: apples, cinnamon and that wonderful smell of chicken and dressing. He grew up with that smell during the holidays. He thought nothing could compare to his mom's apple pie—until he discovered sex. That pretty much put Mom's apple pie in second place. Today he was going to have both and life couldn't get any more perfect than that.

"I'll set the table," Mariel offered.

Elaine stared at her. "There's hay in your hair."

"Oh." She reached up to feel for it.

Gray removed it with a big smile.

"Where's Chloe?" Elaine asked.

"She had to talk to Colonel Bob," Gray said, carrying plates to the table.

"Is she jumping his fences?"

"Like a deer."

"Oh, my. Bob doesn't like that."

"Don't worry, Mom. I think Chloe has the colonel wrapped around her little finger."

"Yeah. He does seem to have a soft spot for her."

Mariel folded napkins while Gray placed his mom's good silver on the table. Chloe breezed in and positioned a piece of white paper on the tree.

"What's that?" Gray asked.

"I went to see Colonel Bob to ask how much I owed him for drawing up the divorce papers. He wrote a figure on a piece of paper." She pointed to the tree. "That's it—a fat zero. I told him that wasn't fair and I owed him something. He said Christmas dinner would just about cover it, so I invited him. We have to set another plate. I know Gran has plenty and he's all alone. The trainers and riders aren't even there today."

"That was very nice," Elaine said. "I should have thought of it."

"Yes," Gray and Mariel agreed together.

Chloe pointed to the paper again. "That's for charity."

Mariel hugged her. "That's wonderful."

"It's a wonderful Christmas, isn't it?"

Gray wrapped his arms around both of them. "Yes. It sure is."

The colonel arrived and brought flowers and a bottle of wine. Chloe inundated him with questions about horses and he patiently answered each one while they ate their delicious meal. Gray and Mariel did the dishes while Elaine and Chloe entertained the colonel in the living room.

Chloe was explaining about the angels when the phone rang. Gray picked it up, assuming it was someone wanting to wish them a Merry Christmas. But it wasn't. It was the FBI. A chill slid down his spine as he listened to the story. He assured the agent he'd be there as soon as he could.

Mariel heard the last part and turned her attention from Chloe to Gray. He couldn't be leaving, could he? Not on Christmas Day. They hadn't had enough time.

"I've got to go. It's an emergency."

The silence in the room was deafening.

"No." Chloe broke the quiet. "Christmas isn't over. You promised, Daddy."

"I'm sorry."

"No, you're not. You're leaving."

"I'll…"

"Don't say you'll make it up to me because you can't."

"Chloe, this is a life-or-death situation and I have to go, but I will be back."

Chloe flopped down in a chair. "Doesn't matter. We were going to talk about my school—that doesn't matter, either."

"Your mother's going to enroll you in your old school after the holidays and we'll make adjustments to be more involved in your life."

Mariel froze. This was what they'd talked about before last night, before they made love. Now everything had changed— for her, but evidently not for him. Why wasn't he telling Chloe they were going to be a family again? It's what she wanted. But evidently it looked like his job still came first.

Gray reached down and kissed Chloe. She didn't respond.

"Baby girl, you need to make an angel of trust for that tree. You have to trust me to make all this right."

Chloe still didn't answer, just kicked at the rug.

His eyes caught hers and her heart stilled. He was leaving. "I'll call as soon as I can." He kissed her briefly, hugged his mother and shook the colonel's hand. Then he was gone.

Mariel felt the bottom of her stomach give way to a lonely, empty feeling. After last night, she had so many hopes. Her hand touched her lips. She could feel his touch, his breath. Last night had been good for him, too. Maybe she should trust him. Maybe…

She caught sight of her daughter's face and her heart broke.

The colonel got to his feet. "Chloe, sometimes you have to give as well as take. That's what life's all about. You had a wonderful Christmas, so be thankful and grateful. Your mom and gran are still here and everyone loves you. Some kids don't have much of anything, at any time of year. Some are lonely and hurting."

"I know, and thank you for trying to help me." She jumped up and ran to her room, banging the door shut.

Chloe found her journal and began to write.

The truth: my parents are not getting back together. I thought it was going to happen. I really did. I prayed for it and believed in the magic of Christmas. My dad is gone and my mom will leave soon. I'll be shuffled around like a bag of dirty laundry. Nothing's changed. I hate them. I hate everything.

Tears fell on the page and she grabbed the journal and threw it into the trash can. Their wonderful Christmas dissipated with every tear.

Chapter Eight

Mariel said goodbye to the colonel and went after Chloe. She was lying on her bed, crying and holding on to Buffy.

Mariel sat beside her. "I'm still here. Doesn't that count for anything?"

"You'll leave soon. You always do."

That hurt-little-girl voice triggered her motherly instincts and she knew she couldn't let Chloe manipulate them with tears or threats of divorce. "Sit up, Chloe. We need to talk."

Something in Mariel's voice must have gotten through because Chloe sat up without a word of protest, brushing tears away. Buffy curled up on a pillow and went to sleep.

"It's your father's job to protect people. That's what he does and he's very good at it. For him to leave us so quickly, someone's life has to be in danger. He wouldn't go for any other reason. Do you understand that?"

As Mariel listened to her own words, she heard the truth in them. Something had happened to take Gray away from them, but he would be back. Sometimes his work was top secret and he couldn't share details. They had to trust him—just like he'd said.

"Chloe," she prompted when her daughter remained silent.

Chloe dove into her arms. "I'm sorry, Mama."

Mariel held her daughter. "I know you are, baby. After the holidays, I'll enroll you in your old school."

"That's okay. I'll just stay at the new one."

"You haven't made many friends there." Mariel worried that after Chloe's friend Jennifer had left to live in another state she didn't make any new friends—just classmates who were only acquaintances and didn't come to the house.

"No." Chloe sank back on her heels, chewing on her hair. "But I met a girl who goes to Gran's church and she's nice. I like her and was hoping to go to school with her."

"I see." She removed the hair from Chloe's mouth. "We'll talk about this again in a few days."

"Okay."

"Now, we better go help Gran feed the animals."

Chloe wiggled off the bed. "I get to drive the truck."

"Who drives the tractor?"

"Gran does."

"That means I sit on the back of the truck and put out the feed."

Chloe grinned. "Yep."

Mariel cupped her face. "Baby, your father loves you." *And he loves me, too. He just hasn't said it again. But she could wait.*

"I know."

"And I love you."

"Yeah." Chloe grinned again. "I love you, too."

They walked out, but Chloe hurried back. "I forgot something. Be right there."

She fished the journal out of the trash and sat on the bed to write an entry. She scribbled through her last words, then wrote.

Trust: tonight Mama and me are making an angel of trust—just like Daddy said. I'm not giving up because I believe in the spirit of Christmas.

ON THE WAY INTO HOUSTON all Gray could see was Mariel's and Chloe's hurt faces. For their own safety he couldn't tell them what had happened. That still didn't make it easy. The FBI had been keeping an eye on the man who'd threatened Mariel's life and he had turned out to be a lot more than a temporary disturbance. The man, Luther Gribbs, had broken into Mariel's condo, hoping she was at home on Christmas. The alarm went off and the police were there in minutes.

When Gribbs realized Mariel wasn't home, he ran out the front door, but the police were closing in. A couple was helping their five-year-old son ride his new bike down the sidewalk. Gribbs had grabbed the boy and barricaded them inside Mariel's condo.

Gray parked two streets away from the scene and attached his gun to his belt, then he put on his badge and got out. A SWAT team and the FBI had the place sealed off for two blocks. An agent came up to him and they made their way through the crowd to the perimeter.

The SWAT commander shook his hand. "Captain Frank Reison."

"What's the situation?" Gray asked.

"Gribbs won't release the boy. He wants to trade him for your daughter."

Gray swallowed. "He broke in to kill Chloe?"

"That's about it. He says Ms. Crandall convicted his son of a murder he didn't commit. Luther Junior kidnapped, raped and murdered a fifteen-year-old girl. His DNA convicted him. He got the death penalty and he was executed a week ago. Gribbs has always said that if his son died so would Ms. Crandall. I guess he figured he'd surprise them today and kill her and her daughter."

"Oh, God." Gray took a breath. He was so glad they were safe at the ranch. "What's your plan?"

"We have sharpshooters with sights on every window hoping to get a clear shot, but Gribbs stays away from the windows. We need to draw him out. We're hoping Ms. Crandall's husband, or ex-husband, can do that. That's why we called. I know you'd booked time off for the holidays and I sure was hoping to get you instead of Ms. Crandall. She doesn't need to be here."

Gray agreed. "Tell me what you want me to do." Gray saw a young couple across the street and he knew it was the parents of the boy inside. The mother was clinging to the father and stark fear was evident in both of them.

"Talk to him and see if he'll exchange you for the boy. That way, maybe we can get a clear shot as he opens the door."

"Okay." He didn't have to think about it. He knew what he had to do. "But I have to make a phone call first."

"Make it short. We're running out of time."

Gray turned away and pulled out his cell phone, poking out his mother's number. Chloe answered.

"Hi, Daddy. I'm sorry I got so mad. Mama, Gran and me did the feeding and Mama drove the tractor."

"Did she?"

"Sure did. She's a regular ranch woman."

"I love you, baby girl."

"I love you, too. Mama and me are making an angel of trust."

"Good. Can I talk to your mom please?"

Mariel came on the line. "Hi."

Just hearing her voice calmed him. "I'm sorry I had to leave so quickly."

"I was a little hurt, but I knew it had to be something important."

"It is and I wanted to call and say something. I don't think I said it last night."

"What?"

"I love you. I've never stopped loving you."

"Oh, Gray. I love you, too." There was a long pause. "Wait a minute. Why aren't you telling me this in person?"

"Mariel…"

"You're involved in something dangerous and…" Her voice faded away.

"Yes. I'm involved in something dangerous," he told her, unable to lie. "So take care of Chloe and Mom and I'll be back as soon as I can."

"Gray," she said before he could hang up.

"What?"

"Be careful. I love you. I will always love you."

He clicked off and handed the captain his phone, gun and badge. He removed his shirt and they put a bulletproof vest on him and gave him instructions.

"The boy's name is Ryan Clark," the captain said, and Gray took the bullhorn.

"Luther Gribbs, this is Grayson Crandall."

"Who the hell are you?"

"Mariel Todd-Crandall's husband."

"That coldhearted bitch doesn't have a husband."

Gray inhaled deeply, trying to not react. "We're divorced, but we're getting back together. That's why she wasn't home. She was with me."

"Then why isn't she with you now?"

"She had to stop and drop gifts at a friend's house." He was making this up as he went along. "But she's on the way."

"This boy ain't going free until she walks in here with her daughter."

"That may take a while, Gribbs. Why don't you trade the boy for me? Let the boy go."

"No. You're trying to trick me."

"How is he?"

"He won't stop crying and he's starting to get on my nerves."

"Then let's make an exchange. I'll meet you at the front door. Let the boy out and I'll come in. You want Mariel, don't you? If I'm in there, she won't hesitate to follow your instructions."

"I don't know."

"Think about it. I'm the father of her child. She wouldn't want you to hurt me. She'll do whatever you ask."

After a long silence, Luther said, "Okay. You better not have a weapon on you and you better tell those cops to back off. If I see anything out of place, I'll kill you and the boy."

"Fine. I'm coming in." He handed the captain the horn and slowly walked up the sidewalk to the front door with his hands in the air. About twenty feet away, he stopped. Members of the SWAT team were plastered against the outside brick wall about four feet on both sides of the front door. Out of his peripheral vision he saw other officers and he knew sharpshooters had their sights trained on the door, waiting for an opening. Gray had to give them one.

"Gribbs, send the boy out," he shouted. "I'm here."

The door opened a crack and Gray could hear the boy's sobs. "Let him go," Gray shouted again.

Slowly the crack inched wider, revealing the young boy. He'd cried so much that now he was only making hiccuping sounds. Gray saw the gun pointed at Ryan's head. Suddenly a blood-curdling scream ripped through the silence, diverting attention and blowing the mission to hell. Gribbs raised the gun and reached to jerk Ryan back.

In a split second Gray made a decision. He was close to Ryan so he made a dive for the boy and flipped with an arm around him into the shrubs amid the thunder of gunfire. His head burned from something, but he had Ryan. He felt him sobbing against him, then everything went black.

MARIEL AND CHLOE FINISHED the supper dishes and walked into the living room. Suddenly Mariel felt a chill. She stopped and ran her hands up her arms. The fire burned warmly so she knew it wasn't the temperature. It was something else—a premonition. Something had happened to Gray. She sank down on the sofa and stared at the angel of hope on top of the tree—and hoped for her family's future.

Please let Gray be okay.

Chloe snuggled up to her. "Mama, are you okay?"

"I'm fine," she replied, hugging Chloe and staring into Elaine's concerned eyes. She knew something was wrong, too. But neither would let on to Chloe.

After Elaine and Chloe had gone to bed, Mariel pulled out the sofa bed and curled up with Gray's pillow, his scent still on it. A tear slipped from her eye and her gaze went back to the angel of hope.

Please bring him back.

Chapter Nine

Gray drove over the cattle guard and felt at peace for the first time in a lot of years. He was home. His family was here and they were safe. He intended to keep it that way.

He'd have been home sooner, but he'd busted his head open by hitting a brick wall while rescuing Ryan. After they'd stitched Gray up, he'd called Mariel and told her he was fine. She said she'd been lying in the sofa bed staring at the angel of hope. When he reassured her he'd be home in a few days, she didn't ask a lot of questions.

It was New Year's Eve and he'd made a lot of decisions since he'd left the ranch. He'd given twenty years of his life to law enforcement and decided it was time to be there for his family. This was an easy decision because it was what he really wanted—to be a full-time husband, father and son. His family needed him. He had officially retired as a U.S. Marshal and now planned to be a rancher—a cowboy again.

He hadn't talked it over with Mariel and he was hoping she wouldn't be upset. Driving to the barn, he saw two riders racing toward him, Chloe and Mariel. Chloe sailed over the fence with ease and he watched in amazement as Mariel followed suit.

Chloe jumped off Flash and sprinted toward him. "Daddy,

Daddy," she shouted, throwing herself into his arms. "I missed you. I love you."

He held his precious child like a newborn baby, realizing how valuable his time was with his daughter. Soon she'd be leaving home, making a life of her own. "I love you, too, baby girl."

Mariel dismounted and ran to Gray. He let go of Chloe and caught her, holding her so tight that his arms ached.

"You're okay. You're okay," she cried, trailing her fingers through his hair, then she touched the wound. "Oh."

"A few stitches, that's all." He captured her lips and kissed her deeply.

Chloe stepped back and smiled. "I gotta go open the gate for Gran." She swung on to Flash and was gone.

After a moment, Gray broke the kiss, grabbed the reins of Mariel's horse, and they walked into the barn. He unsaddled the horse and let her loose in the pasture. Then he took Mariel's hand and sat on a bale of hay with her on his lap.

"Are you sure you're okay?" She ran her fingers through his hair again.

"Yes. I had a bad headache for a couple of days, but I'm going to be fine."

"What happened?"

He told her the whole story.

The blood drained from her face. "He was going to kill me and Chloe?"

"He was determined to kill somebody."

"He's dead?"

"Yes. He started firing when I grabbed Ryan and the SWAT team took him out pretty quick."

"How's Ryan and his family?"

"I stopped by there before I came home. They let him out

of the hospital two days ago. He's still scared, but he's scheduled to see a counselor three times a week. His parents are
going to do all they can to help him get over this."

"I'm glad." She rested her head on his shoulder. "I'll call
them when we get to the house."

"You won't be able to go back to the condo for a while.
The SWAT team did a number on the door, windows and
walls. I had a new door and windows put in, but the inside
needs a lot of work. I really rather you didn't go back there."

She stroked his face. "I've been doing a lot of thinking."

"Me, too."

"Chloe needs me and I'm thinking about resigning. It was
my dad's dream for me to be a U.S. Attorney and I wanted to
please him. But you really have to have a cutthroat instinct to
deal with these hardened criminals. I realized I don't have it. I'm
not putting my child's life in danger again. I can't live like that."

She raised her head to look at him. "Chloe's met a friend, and
you know how hard it's been for her to make friends since Jennifer left. Of course, the trauma in our lives didn't help, either.
But she wants to go to the Sealy school and I think she should."

"Do you?"

"And I'm thinking of opening a law office here to be home
when Chloe needs me."

He smiled. "Did I ever tell you we think alike?"

"What do you mean?"

He told her what he'd done and she wasn't upset at all. She
kissed his cheek, his stitches, his nose, then his mouth. They drew
apart when Elaine drove the truck into the barn. Elaine crawled
out and hurried to her son. Gray stood and embraced his mom.

"You're home, son."

He decided to get right to the point. "How would you feel
about me taking over the ranch?"

"I'd call that the best Christmas present." Elaine smiled. "The ladies at the church are getting together a trip to London and I just might go."

Gray nodded. "Whatever you want to do. It's time to enjoy yourself."

Chloe jumped off Flash and danced around the barn. "Yay! Yay! Yay! We're going to be a family again. Hooray!" Suddenly she stopped and stared at her parents. "That's what this means, doesn't it?"

"Yes, baby girl. That's what this means. We'll be here for you around the clock so you're going to have to walk the line."

Chloe made a face. "We might have to talk about that."

Mariel and Gray laughed.

Elaine glanced at her watch. "Oh. We better go, sweetpea. It's getting late."

"Okay, Gran. I'm right behind you as soon as I put Flash in the pasture." Chloe gave her parents quick kisses and led her horse away.

"Where are they going? It's getting dark," Gray said.

"Bob has invited them to a New Year's dance at the VFW hall and Elaine is very excited about it. I promised to do her nails and we've been shopping for shoes all week. She's wearing the dress we gave her for Christmas."

"Wow. Bob's taking her dancing?"

"He asked Chloe and me, too."

He looked into her eyes. "Do you want to go?"

"No. I hadn't planned on going. I was staying home, waiting for you to return."

"But we can go if you want."

"Think about it. We'd have the house to ourselves, and I'm thinking wine, a lumpy sofa bed and nothing but nothing between us."

He grinned. "I like that plan better." Gray kissed her softly. "We have to do something about the sleeping arrangements and our living quarters in general. The house is too small. We either have to add on or build a new house."

"Let's talk about that tomorrow." She wrapped an arm around his waist. "We have a lot of things to discuss."

"You bet. Like getting married."

"Hmm."

They headed for the house, Bogey and Spence trotting ahead.

"Are you okay with being a rancher's wife—a cowboy's wife?"

"As long as you're the cowboy."

"Always."

"I love you," she whispered on the back porch, and they clung together.

"I love you, too, and let's don't ever forget that again."

CHLOE BURST INTO THE living room and stopped for a second to glance at the angels on the tree, then hurried to her room. She picked up the journal and sat on the bed. Buffy crawled into her lap and she began to write.

The result: It worked. My parents are back together and we're going to live happily ever after or as close as we can get. Colonel Bob said I should be grateful and thankful and I am. The angels brought us the spirit of Christmas and all I had to do was believe in faith, hope, love and a little charity. Love is definitely the greatest, though.

* * * * *

Welcome to the world of American Romance!
Turn the page for excerpts from our December 2005 titles.

OUT OF TOWN BRIDE by Kara Lennox
THE POLICE CHIEF'S LADY by Jacqueline Diamond
A FABULOUS WEDDING by Dianne Castell
SANTA'S TEXAS LULLABY by Cathy Gillen Thacker

We hope you'll enjoy every one of these books!

It's time for some BLOND JUSTICE! This is Kara Lennox's third book in her trilogy about three women who were duped by the same con man. Sonya Patterson's mother has been busy preparing her daughter's wedding—and has no idea the groom-to-be ran off with Sonya's money. Will the blondes finally get their sweet revenge on the evil Marvin? And how long can Sonya pretend that she's going through with the wedding—when she'd rather be married to her longtime bodyguard, John-Michael McPhee? We know you're going to love this funny, fast-paced story!

Airplane seats were way too small, and too crowded together. Sonya Patterson had never thought much about this before, since she'd always flown first class in the past. But this was a last-minute ticket on a no-first-class kind of plane.

She'd also never flown on a commercial airline with her bodyguard, which might explain her current claustrophobia. John-Michael McPhee was a broad-shouldered, well-muscled man, and Sonya was squashed between him and a hyperactive seven-year-old whose mother was fast asleep in the row behind them.

She could smell the leather of McPhee's bomber jacket. He'd had that jacket for years, and every time Sonya saw him in it, her stupid heart gave a little leap. She hated herself for letting him affect her that way. Didn't most women get over their teenage crushes by the time they were pushing thirty?

"I didn't know you were a nervous flier," McPhee said, brushing his index finger over her left hand. Sonya realized she was clutching her armrests as if the plane were about to crash.

What would he think, she wondered, if she blurted out that it wasn't flying that made her nervous, it was being so close to him? Her mother would not approve of Sonya's messy feelings where McPhee was concerned.

Her mother. Sonya's heart ached at the thought of her vibrant mother lying in a hospital bed hooked up to machines. Muffy Lockridge Patterson was one of those women who never stopped, running all day, every day, at full throttle with a To-Do list a mile long. Over the years, Sonya had often encouraged her mother to slow down, relax and cut back on the rich foods. But Muffy seldom took advice from anyone.

Sonya consciously loosened her grip on the armrests when McPhee nudged her again.

"She'll be okay," he said softly. "She was in stable condition when I left."

A comfortable silence passed before McPhee asked, "Are you going to tell me what you were doing in New Orleans with your 'sorority sister'?"

So, he hadn't bought her cover story. But she'd had to come up with something quickly when McPhee had tracked her down hundreds of miles away from where she was supposed to be. She'd already been caught in a bald-faced lie— for weeks she'd been telling her mother she was at a spa in Dallas, working out her pre-wedding jitters.

"I was just having a little fun," she tried again.

"A little fun that got you in trouble with the FBI?"

This is the first book in an exciting new miniseries from Jacqueline Diamond, DOWNHOME DOCTORS. The town of Downhome, Tennessee, has trouble keeping doctors at its small clinic. Advertising an available position at the town's clinic brings more than one candidate for the job, but the townspeople get more than they bargained for when Dr. Jenni Vine is hired, despite Police Chief Ethan Forrest's reservations about her—at least in the beginning!

"Nobody knows better than I do how badly this town needs a doctor," Police Chief Ethan Forrest told the crowd crammed into the Downhome, Tennessee, city council chambers. "But please, not Jenni Vine."

He hadn't meant to couch his objection so bluntly, he mused as he registered the startled reaction of his audience. Six months ago, he'd been so alarmed by the abrupt departure of the town's two resident doctors, a married couple, that he'd probably have said yes to anyone with an M.D. after his or her name.

Worried about his five-year-old son, Nick, who was diabetic, Ethan had suggested that the town advertise for physicians to fill the vacated positions. They'd also recommended that they hire a long-needed obstetrician.

Applications hadn't exactly poured in. Only two had arrived from qualified family doctors, both of whom had toured Downhome recently by invitation. One was clearly superior, and as a member of the three-person search committee, Ethan felt it his duty to say so.

"Dr. Gregory is more experienced and, in my opinion, more stable. He's married with three kids, and I believe he's motivated to stick around for the long term." Although less than ideal in one respect, the Louisville physician took his duties seriously and, Ethan had no doubt, would fit into the community.

"Of course he's motivated!" declared Olivia Rockwell, who stood beside Ethan just below the city council's dais. The tall African-American woman, who was the school principal, chaired the committee. "You told us yourself he's a recovering alcoholic."

"He volunteered the information, along with the fact that he's been sober for a couple of years," Ethan replied. "His references are excellent and he expressed interest in expanding our public health efforts. I think he'd be perfect to oversee the outreach program I've been advocating."

"So would Jenni—I mean Dr. Vine," said the third committee member, Karen Lowell, director of the Tulip Tree Nursing Home. "She's energetic and enthusiastic. Everybody likes her."

"She certainly has an outgoing personality," he responded. On her visit, the California blonde had dazzled people with her expensive clothes and her good humor after being drenched in a thunderstorm, which she seemed to regard as a freak of nature. It probably didn't rain on her parade very often out there in the land of perpetual sunshine, Ethan supposed. "But once the novelty wears off, she'll head for greener pastures and we'll need another doctor."

"So you aren't convinced she'll stay? Is that the extent of your objections?" Olivia asked. "This isn't typical of you, Chief. I'll bet you've got something else up that tailored sleeve of yours."

Ethan was about to pass off her comment as a joke, when he noticed some of the townsfolk leaning forward in their seats with anticipation. Despite being a quiet place best known for dairy farmers and a factory that made imitation antiques, Downhome had an appetite for gossip.

Although Ethan had hoped to avoid going into detail, the audience awaited his explanation. Was he being unfair? True, he'd taken a mild dislike to Dr. Vine's surfer-girl demeanor, but he could get over that. What troubled him was the reason she'd wanted to leave L.A. in the first place.

"You all know I conducted background checks on the candidates," he began. "Credit records, convictions, that sort of thing."

"And found no criminal activities, right?" Karen tucked a curly strand of reddish-brown hair behind one ear.

"That's correct. But I also double-checked with the medical directors at their hospitals." He had a bomb to drop now, so he'd better get it over with.

This is the final book of Dianne Castell's FORTY & FABU-
LOUS trilogy about three women living in Whistlers Bend,
Montana, who are dealing (or not dealing!) with turning forty.
Dixie Carmichael has just had her fortieth birthday, and gotten the best birthday present of all—a second chance at life—
after the ultimate medical scare. One thing she's sure
of—now's the time to start living life the way she's always
wanted it to be!

Dixie Carmichael twisted her fingers into the white sheet as she lay perfectly still on the OR table and tried to remember to breathe. Fear settled in her belly like sour milk. *She was scared!* Bone-numbing, jelly-legged, full-blown-migraine petrified. It wasn't every day her left breast got turned into a giant pincushion.

She closed her eyes, not wanting to look at the ultrasound machine or think about the biopsy needle or anything else in the overly bright sterile room that would determine if the lump was really bad news.

She clenched her teeth so they wouldn't chatter, then prayed for herself and all women who ever went, or would go, through this. The horror of waiting to find out the diagnosis was more terrifying than her divorce or wrapping her Camaro around a tree rolled into one.

God, let me out of this and I'll change. I swear it. No more pity parties over getting dumped by Danny for that Victoria's Secret model, no more comfort junk food, no more telling everyone how to live their lives and not really living her own, and if that meant leaving Whistlers Bend, she'd suck it up and do it and quit making excuses.

"We're taking out the fluid now," the surgeon said. "It's clear."

Dixie's eyes shot wide open. She swallowed, then finally managed to ask, "Meaning?"

The surgeon stayed focused on what she was doing, but the news was good. Dixie could tell—she'd picked up being able to read people from waiting tables at the Purple Sage restaurant for three years and dealing with happy, way-less-than-happy and everything-in-between customers. *Oh, how she wished she were at the Purple Sage now.*

The surgeon continued. "Meaning the lump in your breast is a cyst. I'll send the fluid we drew off to the pathologist to be certain, but there's no indication the lump was anything more than a nuisance."

Nuisance! A nuisance was a telemarketer, a traffic ticket, gaining five pounds! But the important thing was, she'd escaped. She said another prayer for the women who wouldn't escape. Then she got dressed and left the hospital, resisting the urge to turn handsprings all the way to her car. Or maybe she did them, she wasn't sure.

She could go home. In one hour she'd be back in Whistlers Bend. Her life still belonged to her, and not doctors and hospitals and pills and procedures. She fired up her Camaro and sat for a moment, appreciating the familiar idle of her favorite car while staring out at the flat landscape of Billings, Montana. This was one of the definitive moments when life smacked her upside the head and said, *Dixie, old girl, get your ass in gear.*

You've wanted action, adventure, hair-raising experiences as long as you can remember. Now's the time to make them happen!

Welcome back to Laramie, Texas, and a whole new crop of McCabes! In this story, prankster Riley McCabe is presented with three abandoned children one week before Christmas. Thinking it's a joke played on him by Amanda Witherspoon, he comes to realize the kids really do need his help. Watch out for Cathy Gillen Thacker's next book, *A Texas Wedding Vow,* in April 2006.

Amanda Witherspoon had heard Riley McCabe was returning to Laramie, Texas to join the Laramie Community Hospital staff, but she hadn't actually *seen* the handsome family
physician until Friday afternoon when he stormed into the
staff lounge in the pediatrics wing.

Nearly fourteen years had passed, but his impact on her was
the same. Just one look into his amber eyes made her pulse
race, and her emotions skyrocket. He had been six foot when
he left for college, now he was even taller. Back then he had
worn his sun-streaked light brown hair any which way. Now
the thick wavy strands were cut in a sophisticated fashion,
parted neatly on the left and brushed casually to the side. He
looked solid and fit, mouthwateringly sexy, and every inch the
kind of grown man who knew exactly who he was and what
he wanted out of life. The kind not to be messed with. Amanda
thought the sound of holiday music playing on the hospital
sound system and the Christmas tree in the corner only added
to the fantasy-come-true quality of the situation.

Had she not known better, Amanda would have figured
Riley McCabe's return to her life would have been the Christmas present to beat all Christmas presents, meant to liven up

her increasingly dull and dissatisfying life. But wildly exciting things like that never happened to Amanda.

"Notice I'm not laughing," Riley McCabe growled as he passed close enough for her to inhale the fragrance of soap and brisk, wintry cologne clinging to his skin.

"Notice," Amanda returned dryly, wondering what the famously mischievous prankster was up to now, "neither am I."

Riley marched toward her, jaw thrust out pugnaciously, thick straight brows raised in mute admonition. "I would have figured we were beyond all this."

Amanda had hoped that would be the case, too. After all, she was a registered nurse, he a doctor. But given the fact that the Riley McCabe she recalled had been as full of mischief as the Texas sky was big, that had been a dangerous supposition to make. "Beyond all what?" she repeated around the sudden dryness of her throat. As he neared her, all the air left her lungs in one big whoosh.

"The practical jokes! But you just couldn't resist, could you?"

Amanda put down the sandwich she had yet to take a bite of and took a long sip of her diet soda. "I have no idea what you're talking about," she said coolly. Unless this was the beginning of yet another ploy to get her attention?

"Don't you?" he challenged, causing another shimmer of awareness to sift through her.

Deciding that sitting while he stood over her gave him too much of a physical advantage, she pushed back her chair and rose slowly to her feet. She was keenly aware that he now had a good six inches on her, every one of them as bold and masculine as the set of his lips. "I didn't think you were due to start working here until January." She sounded way more casual than she felt.

He stood in front of her, arms crossed against his chest, legs braced apart, every inch of him taut and ready for action. "I'm not."

"So?" She ignored the intensity in the long-lashed amber eyes that threatened to throw her off balance. "How could I possibly play a prank on you if I didn't think you were going to be here?"

"Because," he replied, "you knew I was going to start setting up my office in the annex today."

Amanda sucked in a breath. "I most certainly did not!" she insisted. Although she might have had she realized he intended to pick up right where they had left off, all those years ago. Matching wits and wills. The one thing she had never wanted to cede to the reckless instigator was victory of any kind.

Riley leaned closer, not stopping until they were practically close enough to kiss. "Listen to me, Amanda, and listen good. Playing innocent is not going to work with me. And neither," he warned, even more forcefully, "is your latest gag."

Amanda regarded him in a devil-may-care way designed to get under his skin as surely as he was already getting under hers. "I repeat," she spoke as if to the village idiot, "I have no idea what you are talking about, Dr. McCabe. Now, do you mind? I only have a forty-five-minute break and I'd like to eat my lunch."

He flashed her an incendiary smile that left her feeling more aware of him than ever. "I'll gladly leave you alone just as soon as you collect them."

Amanda blinked, more confused than ever. "Collect who?" she asked incredulously.

Riley walked back to the door. Swung it open wide. On the other side was the surprise of Amanda's life.

Home For The Holidays!

Indulge in Leah Vale's great holiday recipe

Family Fattigmann
Traditional Norwegian Christmas Cookies

Have at least one beloved family member or friend within shouting distance. The more the merrier.

6 egg yolks	1 tbsp whiskey
3 egg whites	2 1/2 cups flour
6 tbsp sugar	Vegetable oil for frying
6 tbsp canned milk	Powdered sugar

(and no nipping from the bottle—there's hot oil to follow!)

Beat egg yolks until creamy. Add sugar, milk and whiskey. In a separate bowl, beat egg whites until stiff, then add to egg mixture. Add flour to make soft dough. Chill in refrigerator. No, it's not time for that hot whiskey toddy, yet! When dough is almost ready, heat the vegetable oil in a deep saucepan. It should sizzle, but not smoke. Once dough is stiff, roll out until very thin—about 1/16 inch thick—on a lightly floured surface. Use a floured knife to cut dough into diamond shapes approximately 2 by 1 inch. Cut a slit lengthwise in the center of each diamond and pull one end through the slot to make a sort of knot. In batches, deep-fry the cookies until they are golden brown, then drain on paper towels and cool. Place cookies in a clean paper bag with some powdered sugar, roll the top closed and then dance around the kitchen shaking the bag. Store cookies in airtight containers.

eHARLEQUIN.com

The Ultimate Destination for Women's Fiction
The ultimate destination for women's fiction.
Visit eHarlequin.com today!

GREAT BOOKS:
- We've got something for everyone—and at great low prices!
- Choose from new releases, backlist favorites, Themed Collections and preview upcoming books, too.
- Favorite authors: Debbie Macomber, Diana Palmer, Susan Wiggs and more!

EASY SHOPPING:
- Choose our convenient "bill me" option. No credit card required!
- Easy, secure, 24-hour shopping from the comfort of your own home.
- Sign-up for free membership and get $4 off your first purchase.
- Exclusive online offers: FREE books, bargain outlet savings, hot deals.

EXCLUSIVE FEATURES:
- Try Book Matcher—finding your favorite read has never been easier!
- Save & redeem Bonus Bucks.
- Another reason to love Fridays— Free Book Fridays!

Shop online
at www.eHarlequin.com today!

INTBB204R

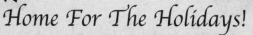

Home For The Holidays!

Receive a FREE Christmas Collection
containing 4 books by bestselling authors

STELLA CAMERON — An Angel In Time

VICKI LEWIS THOMPSON — Tis the Season

ANNETTE BROADRICK — Daddy's Angel

RACHEL LEE — An Officer and a Gentleman

**Harlequin American Romance and Silhouette Special Edition
invite you to celebrate Home For The Holidays by offering you this
exclusive offer valid only in Harlequin American Romance and
Silhouette Special Edition books this November.**

To receive your FREE Christmas Collection, send us 3 (three) proofs of
purchase of Harlequin American Romance or Silhouette Special Edition
books to the addresses below.

Home For The Holidays!

While there are many variations of this recipe, here is Tina Leonard's favorite!

GOURMET REINDEER POOP

Mix 1/2 cup butter, 2 cups granulated sugar, 1/2 cup milk and 2 tsp cocoa together in a large saucepan.

Bring to a boil, stirring constantly; boil for 1 minute.

Remove from heat and stir in 1/2 cup peanut butter, 3 cups oatmeal (not instant) and 1/2 cup chopped nuts (optional).

Drop by teaspoon full (larger or smaller as desired) onto wax paper and let harden.

They will set in about 30-60 minutes.

These will keep for several days without refrigerating, up to 2 weeks refrigerated and 2-3 months frozen.

Pack into resealable sandwich bags and attach the following note to each bag.

I woke up with such a scare when I heard Santa call...
"Now dash away, dash away, dash away all!"
I ran to the lawn and in the snowy white drifts,
those nasty reindeer had left "little gifts."
I got an old shovel and started to scoop,
neat little piles of "Reindeer Poop!"
But to throw them away seemed such a waste,
so I saved them, thinking you might like a taste!
As I finished my task, which took quite a while,
Old Santa passed by and he sheepishly smiled.
And I heard him exclaim as he was in the sky...
"Well, they're not potty trained, but at least they can fly!"